PHILLY AMATEURS

Books by Richard E. Peck

FICTION

Philly Amateurs

Strategy of Terror

Dead Pawn

Something for Joey

Final Solution

NON-FICTION

All the Courses in the Kingdom:
An American Plays at the Birthplace of Golf

The New Mexico Experience:
A Confluence of Cultures

Poems: Nathaniel Hawthorne

RICHARD E.
PECK

University of New Mexico Press
ALBUQUERQUE

F

Printed in the United States of America

YEAR PRINTING
12 11 10 09 08 07 06 1 2 3 4 5 6 7

Library of Congress Cataloging-in-Publication Data

Peck, Richard E.
Philly amateurs / Richard E. Peck.
p. cm.
ISBN-13: 978-0-8263-3939-3 (alk. paper)
ISBN-10: 0-8263-3939-5 (alk. paper)
1. Automobile theft—Fiction. 2. Occasional criminals—Fiction. I. Title.
PS3566.E253P48 2006
813'.54—dc22

2006002625

Book design and composition by Damien Shay
Body type is Trump Mediaeval 10/14
Display is Skyline and Impact

This one's for

Bob & Wanda
Judie, and
Larry & Micky

MONDAY

At 8:29 AM on a mid-October Monday, Mike Bradley walked head-high proud into the posh conference room of Philadelphia's Heritage Old-Line Fidelity Insurance Company, poised to conquer the new underwriters' training program. By noon he was sagging and sick of the job. His first job. Not only his first since graduating from Temple University some nine weeks earlier. His first ever, in all his twenty-four years.

At 12:02 PM he escaped from the Heritage Building into Indian summer, hurried along Chestnut Street and turned down Broad to the chrome-wrapped glass showroom of Yamamoto Motors. He picked up a Japanese fragment of the American Dream: his new wheels, dealer-prepped, waxed and waiting for him—the gleaming red Honda Prelude he had bought last Friday, minutes after winning the job at Heritage. First job, first new car.

His live-in girlfriend, Lee Schaeffer, would spit nails when she learned that he'd surrendered to middle-class mores and gone to work. He couldn't conceal his guilty secret for long. She always read him with some kind of secret-piercing device nature had given her. If only he could divert her. . . . The Prelude—lacquered candy-apple red, gray leather interior and CD player, sunroof and spoiler—was a splash of sex and freedom right off the sun-sparkled beaches of TV ads. It might dazzle her enough for Mike to apologize for his unspeakable descent into respectability.

And it might not.

At 12:27, he got lucky and found a parking place on Sansom Street near 17th, only three blocks from the Heritage Building. Even luckier, there was an hour left on the meter. He locked the car, checked the whitewalls for scuffmarks, and strutted into Meyer's Deli for lunch.

At 12:54, he stepped out of Meyer's into more luck.

There are two kinds.

From half a block away, he watched someone steal his new car.

A gray moving van backed into the now-empty parking space ahead of the Honda. The back doors of the van swung open, its tailgate descended on pneumatic tubes. A pair of forklift tines inched out of the tailgate and slipped under the Honda. Then, while crowds of shoppers and office workers on lunch hour jostled past unconcerned, the sparkling Honda Prelude—sunshine spotlighting its pristine brilliance—rose slowly and majestically into the air and disappeared into the black cavern of the truck's huge trailer, dimming like a fading dream as it entered the darkness. Hinged doors swung shut again. Clicked. The guilty truck, and its innocent contents, rolled away from the curb.

"Hey! My car!" Mike dashed into the street, caromed off the side of a rusted Pinto, and cut in front of a cab, whose driver stood on his brakes and lurched headfirst over the steering wheel into the windshield. It hurt.

"Stop him, somebody stop him!" Mike shouted as he burst through a knot of pedestrians stumbling to escape his charge. The gray truck seemed to pause for an instant, teasing him, before it turned the corner with a farewell belch of black exhaust. Hope spurred Mike into longer strides, but he bounced off a woman whose rolled umbrella shot from under her arm and between his knees to send him sprawling.

"Hoodlum! Why'ntcha watch—"

"Excuse me. I've got to—"

"Mugger! Rape! Rape!"

Mike scrambled to his feet and careened to the end of the block, outdistancing the woman's shouts. When he rounded the corner the moving van had vanished. He saw only a policeman ticketing a motorcycle parked on the sidewalk. "Did you, uh," he said. "Uh—did you see a truck go by?"

The temperature stood at eighty-four humid degrees in Center City Philadelphia, the last gasp of a dying summer. Patrolman Warren Cappel had indigestion, three hours to go on a five-hour shift ticketing cars in this sweltering heat, and a rash that made him duck into a doorway every few minutes to scratch his crotch like a major league batter unaware of the TV camera. Officer Cappel was not in a good mood. He glared at Mike.

A cab driver with a bloody nose shouted unintelligible curses and waved a one-finger salute as he screeched past.

"A truck, I said. Did you see a truck go by?"

Cappel glanced up and down the street. He counted nine trucks in various stages of going by. In fact he saw no truck that wasn't going by. "They tend to do that," he said. "Go by, I mean."

"A gray moving van, with no markings on it."

"Kind of in a plain gray wrapper, was it?"

"A moving van, dammit! It picked up my car!" Mike dashed into the street to shout at no one. "Hey!"

Cappel chewed his pencil tip for a moment. "Well, maybe it was love. You know, truck meets car, they do some automotive humping, raise up a bunch of motor scooters."

Mike dropped from his toes and stopped scanning the flow of westbound traffic. He turned to look at the cop. "I mean it, now. The truck backed up to my car, picked it up, and drove off."

"Ahhh, I get it. You want to report a car heist. Or hoist. Not a 'vehicular elopement.' So what you do is, you trot your ass over to The Roundhouse and—"

"I want to know if you saw the damn truck! By now it's in Delaware!"

Cappel sighed. "Was it a big car or a little car?"

"What, mine? It's a Honda Prelude. Or it was."

"It was? What is it now?"

Mike resigned. "A Honda Prelude."

"That's a little car." Cappel scratched a note on the pad he carried. "Would you say the truck had any trouble picking it up?" He held his pencil poised. The resignation on his face implied that he could play the game as long as Bradley could. He wasn't enjoying it, but he could play.

"What do you mean, 'trouble'?"

"I'm assuming it wasn't a tow truck, is that right?"

"No, a moving van. I told you."

"See? Then if it wasn't a tow truck, it couldn't tow your car and had to pick it up, like so." He gestured, palms up. "And I could tell the chief—he'll want to hear all about this personally—I could tell the chief we're looking for a regular truck. A gray, regular truck, only with probably a hernia."

"You don't believe me."

Cappel backed away a step, his face pained. "Awww, why'd you go and say that? Here we was having such a good time and all. The chief likes these stories. He doesn't get out like he used to, and he lives like what you call a 'vicarious' life. Sometimes I say to him, 'nothing special today, couple ax-murders, run-of-the-mill mayhem,' you know? But today! Today I'm going to like run right back there to his office and say, 'you should have been on the street when this truck picked up a car. And then run off with it!' Oh, the chief, he'll love that one."

"There he is!" An umbrella came from nowhere to poke Mike in the chest. Holding it was a red-faced woman of sixty, her ribbon-decked yellow straw hat askew over one eye. "Officer, arrest him. He attacked me!"

Stunned, Mike stared at her. He turned to deny everything but saw it wasn't necessary. Officer Cappel was staring up at the smog-masked shimmering penny of a sun, mumbling to himself. And scratching.

"Are you going to arrest him, officer? I've got witnesses."

"Buzz off, lady, before I tag you for soliciting."

"My car..." Mike let the comment die. He saw mania in Cappel's eye and surrendered. "Right. I'll go to the station."

The woman shouted, "No you don't!" She hefted her umbrella. "Not until I—"

"Lady, have you got a license for that thing?"

"A what?"

"Because the Reverend Schwartz here could press charges."

Glancing from the patrolman to Mike and back, she said, "Reverend Schwartz?"

"Bless you, Sister." Mike shook her limp hand and ducked around the corner.

No one in the sweating crowd paid the slightest attention. They brushed past him seeking air-conditioned offices or stores.

He headed back toward the Heritage Building and his afternoon training session, counting the ways to confess his screw-up to Lee. Counting the ways didn't take long. There weren't many. Somewhere between none and one. And when he turned the corner onto Chestnut and read the engraved brass plaque above the double doors of the building—"Heritage Old-Line Fidelity Insurance. We Care"—another problem occurred to him. Explaining to Lee that he still owed sixty payments (out of sixty) on a car she'd never seen would be tough enough. She'd be even less happy at the news that he hadn't yet insured the damn thing!

Between the birth of Michael Alan Bradley and the theft of his new Honda stretched twenty-four powder-blue years of cloudless sky. He inherited from his mother a quick, perceptive mind, from his father a world-class bent for laziness, traits that combined to make him a small success in the only way that mattered to him. Mike Bradley had never been forced to work. At anything.

His childhood glowed a pleasant golden haze in memory. His father Phil spent five days a week on the road as a salesman for a detergent wholesaler. His mother sat at the Formica-topped table in the aromatic clutter of their kitchen and read while the cookies baked. Mike raised himself on the green, shaded streets of Philadelphia's Mount Airy section, with fund-raising excursions into the neighboring ghetto of Germantown. His quick eye and quicker hand made him gifted at matching coins. He read people well, played acceptable tennis, shot a good stick of pool, all skills that could be turned to cash. His weekly income in high school seldom dropped below $30—enough to buy milkshakes and magazines, not enough to scare off the marks who lost the $30 to him. From age thirteen on, Mike Bradley might have been called a gambler, by some. They would have been wrong. He had never gambled, if by "gambling" you mean risking cash on a contest whose outcome is in doubt. He never bet on anything or anyone but himself, and he knew his own skills and limitations very well.

Both parents were killed in an accident the week of Mike's high school graduation. A private plane departing Philadelphia's International Airport had engine failure and crashed into the Bradleys' three-year-old Chevy station wagon traveling Interstate 95 and hurled it into the ochre sludge of Tinicum Marsh across the road.

Days later, Michael Alan Bradley enlisted in the U.S. Army. He didn't want to be a soldier, visit exotic foreign lands, meet interesting new people, and kill them. He wanted the GI Bill to pay his way to college.

Each morning in basic training he rose ten minutes before reveille to stand shivering in the pre-dawn twilight and carefully, fastidiously, from a safely dry-footed distance, wet the bed. It took four boring weeks for the army to process his medical discharge, another month to complete the paperwork necessary to start the flow of veteran's benefits, and that September he began attending Temple University on the GI Bill.

In class, he listened. Few enough students do. His attentiveness taught him a secret apparently unknown to his instructors. In Freshman English he read an essay by John Stuart Mill. In Elementary Economics he read an essay by John Stuart Mill. In History of Philosophy he read an essay by John Stuart Mill. All the same essay, by the same John Stuart Mill, a coincidence that seemed to elude the professors teaching those three separate classes.

Mike came to understand that what he heard in one classroom could decorate exams he took in another. For the next five years he served as a conduit, carrying information and opinions from one professor to another, and much of the information lodged with him in passing. He wasn't so much a student as a synthesizer (you can't major in Synthesis). This method earned him exceptional grades, and it left free the time he needed to develop card-playing skills—poker and sheepshead, euchre, pinochle, of course, even hearts—skills that fed him.

After a year the army discovered that Mike had not served long enough to earn his GI Bill allotment. Some lieutenant wrote him a nasty letter demanding that he return all moneys illicitly received. He ignored it. A major wrote and threatened legal steps. Mike ignored him. A colonel took "Official Action," and after a flurry of unintelligible forms and misapplication of contradictory policies, all contact ceased before the case reached a general. The resolution remained pending.

For the next three years, while the resolution continued to pend, they sent him not one government check a month, but two.

Anonymously, he turned himself in, hoping to generate another check a month. It didn't work, but it was worth a try.

Halfway through his senior year he moved in with Lee Schaeffer, just before she dropped out of Temple and bought a used loom. He also moved in with her father Harry, as it happened, but he could overlook Harry's presence most of the time. The two men had something in common besides their differing kinds of love for Lee. As Mike had been, Harry remained—a ward of the government. Like Mike, Harry was a happy recipient of a monthly check from Uncle Sugar, his a disability check earned by a single-day siege of bronchitis that brightened the morning he was discharged from the Navy in 1986. Combining Harry's check with what Lee generated selling wool ponchos she wove and what Mike could hustle, the three got along very well. Mike Bradley's life was a bowl of plums.

Until lightning struck.

It happened in Ruggiero's Drugstore, where Mike had gone to pick up a pint of Ruggiero's home-brewed allergy medicine for Harry. Standing between the Roi Tan cigars and the Hallmark cards, waiting for Ruggiero to draw a pint from the keg in the basement, Mike saw a man enter with his four-year-old son holding his hand.

The pair sat at the marble-topped fountain counter and shared a strawberry sundae. Nothing very striking about that, all right off a Norman Rockwell cover, yet it hit Mike then: he wanted kids. A family. That meant talking Lee Schaeffer into A PERMANENT COMMITMENT.

Maybe even marriage. It meant responsibility, finding a job. Cause and effect.

Finding a job, how tough could it be? It was leading Lee to marriage and motherhood that flouted the odds. In the eight months they'd been living together she'd come to like the arrangement more and more. "Why break up a happy home?" she asked, whenever Mike reached the verge of proposing. "Marriage is for old people."

Mike always agreed, until that sentimental moment in Ruggiero's Drugstore. Shazam! Lightning struck. "Get married," came a still, small voice.

That morning's *Inquirer* listed 314 employment opportunities, "sales" the most plentiful at 183. Weren't sales skills the very skills Mike had lived by all his life? He went home, borrowed Harry Schaeffer's suit (while fending off Lee's suspicious questions) and went for an interview with the Heritage Old-Line Fidelity Insurance Company.

The second-floor foyer of the Heritage Building was an acre of maroon carpet surrounded by worm-woody and gall-scarred oak paneling. It was staid, solid, dependable, comforting in its conservatism, and dull. Off the foyer was the personnel director's contrasting cubicle—all glass, chrome, and plastic, way station to the good life, or comfort to anyone nostalgic for Howard Johnson's turnpike rest stops. Mike shrugged himself lower in the white plastic cone some perverse designer had claimed was a chair.

"What makes you think you found the right position?" the personnel manager asked.

Bradley began to recite. He had learned, as most college graduates do, what sort of answers corporate recruiters expect to hear. While the automatic responses purred from him, a part of his mind watched his performance. The image was fine: Harry Schaeffer's suit fit well. He wore a new white shirt and a hideous floral tie that would revert from high stylishness to its natural state as upholstery or a piece of drapery when reps and solid-color knits came back into favor. The attaché case he balanced on his knees was so new that it still wore a price tag on one corner winking white.

He peeled the tag off and stuck it under the edge of his chair. Beside a wad of gum. A soft wad of gum. Another applicant had just been there.

"I know, I know," the man interrupted Mike's recital. "We all want a chance for advancement. But . . ." He gave a wink that said, cut the snowjob, kid—here comes the big question. "Why insurance?"

Without choking, Mike said, "I like to help people."

The personnel director's lips formed the same five words, one at a time. He leaned back, straightened a paperclip, and began to pick his teeth. "You're the first one who's told me that all morning. Do you believe it?"

"Do I have to?"

"Where'd you pick it up?"

"In a brochure I read out in the lobby while I was waiting."

Head cocked, paperclip gouging away, the man stared for a moment. "All right," he said. "You'll do."

Mike felt his shoulders slump as tension relaxed. The chair sucked him two inches deeper into its conical point. Through the glass partition he watched a gaggle of secretaries leaving for lunch.

". . . training program Monday morning. Understand?"

"Monday, yes. Morning." Mike struggled out of the chair and took back the résumé held out to him. "I'll be here. Nine sharp."

"Eight thirty."

"Right. Eight thirty." He reached out to shake hands and seal their bargain but the personnel manager was staring cross-eyed at something green impaled on the point of his paperclip toothpick. Mike left.

On Chestnut Street he looked back to examine the Heritage Building. A former bank, it occupied a quarter of the block, imposing in its marble pillars and white-shuttered windows. Above the double doors of the entrance was a tasteful brass plaque: "Heritage Old-Line Fidelity Insurance. We Care." His company.

Delighted with himself, with the sunshine that warmed the morning, with the long-legged secretaries tripping along the sidewalk in giggling groups, he balanced his attaché case atop a wire trash basket and opened it. He slipped the résumé inside, traded it for two pieces of rye bread and a can of sardines in mustard sauce, and treated himself to a secret sandwich that vegetarian Lee might never know about. He ate it with no shame at all, savored the mustard-spiced fish flesh (Lee would say), sauntering toward Broad Street, admiring himself in store windows. Mike Bradley, employed. Why not? American breadwinner, like millions of others. He might even come to like it.

Headed toward a subway kiosk, he swerved, stopped, was inspired. No more subways for him! Not with a job lined up and three hundred dollars in savings swelling the pants pocket of Harry Schaeffer's suit. The day demanded a symbol, a mark of the new man Mike Bradley had become.

Three blocks south down Broad was Yamamoto Motors, a Honda agency. Mike walked straight to a salesman's desk, licking mustard off his fingers.

"Yes sir?"

Not "whaddayawant kid?" *Yes sir.*

It made his day.

"Mike Bradley," he said, shaking hands. "I'd like to buy that car." The Prelude nearest them in the showroom was fire-engine-Chinese-eye-popping-definitively red, a gleaming splendor.

"That's what we're here for." The salesman's capped teeth glittered. His nostrils twitched, he glanced around puzzled, thinking for some reason of baseball. His smile crumpled and collapsed. He raised his right hand to smell it and smeared mustard on his nose.

"Let's do the paperwork," Mike said. "I'll pick up the car Monday noon."

And he did pick it up on Monday. Thirty minutes before an unmarked gray moving van picked it up on Sansom Street.

Right onto 19th, right onto the Vine Street Expressway (no trucks allowed on Market Street, midday), and wallowing east toward the Ben Franklin Bridge across the Delaware River into New Jersey, the loaded gray moving van moved. In the darkness of its cavernous cargo area, Mike Bradley's Honda Prelude shone less sparkling red than blood-sullen cranberry.

But then, no one could see it. It sat secured by canvas webbing straps stretched taut to eyebolts in the floor fore and aft, left and right. Immobilized, the captive automobile rattled toward a change of life.

"Back to the shop?" the van driver asked.

Seated beside him, George Zordich shook his head and tapped the clipboard he held in one meaty hand. "Lester wants this one painted," he said. "Beige."

"What the hell's that mean? 'Bayj'?" Jack asked. "You hear women and designer queers say that all the time. 'Bayj.' But—"

"Tan, then, you dumbass. Beige is like a light tan, only creamier."

"Shit, George. Now you're sounding like Lester—'creamy tan.'" He flipped a limp wrist but one glance at his passenger made him blanch. George was pointing a warning finger the size of a hotdog, bun and all. "I didn't mean nothing by that, George. Honest. Whatever you say."

"Whatever Lester says. . . . Take the Honda to Earl Sheib's. Lester says they got a special sale week."

The moving van hit the tilt-up bridge threshold and Jack downshifted to start the shuddering climb up the western incline of the Ben Franklin, passing high above the green breadth of Penn's Landing Park beside the river 170 feet below.

Early Monday afternoon, there were few picnickers in Penn's Landing Park. Here and there an office worker stretched his lunch hour in the sun or walked off the weekend's indulgence—his tie loosened, his belt tight—while Lee Schaeffer wove her jogging route through the casual spectators and traced a passage marked by heads turned in her wake. Beauty draws attention.

A slender vegetarian, Lee radiated vitality and corn-fed good looks—an Iowa cheerleader with California thighs. No matter how she tugged and straightened and rinsed and pressed, her blonde hair hung in soft waves. Her cheeks glowed, on the verge of a blush. Hitchhiking through Wisconsin the summer before she dropped out of Temple, she'd been offered a job by the former PR director of the Wisconsin Cheese Council. Modeling, he said, and he would take the photos. He made the offer as they sat waiting at a traffic light in downtown Oconomowoc, resting his right hand on her thigh, cupping her chin with his left. She bit it.

Mike was different. He marveled at more than her beauty—especially the focus she brought to every task. At her loom she was serene, her fingers bringing life to warp and woof; at the grocer's she "became" the fondled ripeness of each avocado in her hands. And now, today, she jogged.

Not so easy running, pensive, concerned with Mike's behavior these three days—something on his mind, a secret, separating them. A barrier between them. The only man she'd met who didn't need coddling, Mike loved her for her presence, not her beauty but the focus of her life.

"You're always here!" he said in wonder.

The man in sweats and Foster Grants who'd been trailing Lee caught her in the band of cool shadows beneath the bridge approach. She smelled his aftershave, overpowering Old Spice, heard the whistle of each hard-earned breath and the thud of his Nikes drawing near. He leered askance, peering sidelong from behind the cover of his tinted shades.

Fifteen strides to go, Lee estimated; fourteen, thirteen...

She shrugged her shoulders, froze his stare, shook her breasts in rhythmic sway beneath the Olga bra and T-shirt that she wore—seven, six—swerved left, smiling at him—two...and one...and...impact!

With his head turned to watch Lee run, he hit the lamppost in full stride, smacked the ringing metal post with ear and jaw and shoulder and hip and ankle with a clang that celebrated Lee's success. He spun to the ground, stunned.

Scratch one schmuck.

Lee ran on, still thinking of Mike and of the change, the "something new" that threatened what they had. Change. And that meant trouble. She could feel it.

Thirteen of the fifteen Heritage trainees proved their eagerness by beating Mike back to the conference room after lunch that October Monday. When he entered he saw them drifting in muted conversation, wary heads canted toward the leather-padded doors at the front of the room to watch for their training leader's return. His arrival would begin the afternoon session.

Mike shook off his mood. There was nothing he could do till the class ended. He would report the theft of a car with less than twelve miles on the odometer, go home to face Lee, and play it by ear from there. The morning had been filled by a single, dry lecture, and seated at the table with everyone else—all heads turned toward the lectern—Mike had seen a few earlobes or the profiles of trainees across the table from him. That was all.

Collected on their feet this way, they seemed a chorus in cordovans and herringbone, corporate-proper white shirts or semi-risky blue, over in one corner of the room the rebellious grid of tattersall. Button-down collars were back in, and attaché cases had never been out. The soft wink of dyed alligator and black Samsonite dangled knee-high beside each of the men treading with contrived confidence through the deep carpet.

An oval conference table, glistening and redolent of lemon Pledge, filled the center of the room. Twenty chairs circled it, at each place a legal pad and three lethally pointed number two pencils, all sharpened during the lunch break. On the paneled walls of the room hung mottoes—"We Care," prominent beside the padded doors—and at intervals were photographs labeled "Million-A-Year Club," "Auto Underwriters Picnic," "Health Group Group."

Mike leaned close to study a photograph of a vested, leonine executive shaking hands with a cocky kid in pinstripes. A caption beneath the picture read "Mr. Winthrop congratulates Howard Gould (Wharton '91), first in his class. 9/91."

"Know him?" asked a voice at Mike's elbow.

"The guy in the picture? I don't think so."

"Howie Gould. In one year he made division manager. He runs the whole Des Moines office."

"Somebody's got to do it."

"Robert Boyle," the man introduced himself. "Williams."

Mike shook hands with him. "Michael Alan," he said. "Bradley."

"Really?" Boyle smiled. "I had a friend who went to Bradley. Well, not actually a friend, you understand. An acquaintance. Tony Crump, physics major or something. He was—"

"Oh, that's what 'Williams' meant. Your school, not your name."

"My name's Boyle, I said."

"Sorry I'm late," a grating voice interrupted. "We get name tags or something?" A short, stocky man in fringed buckskins and black curls, carrying a large sketchpad under one arm, bounded into the room in mid-sentence, leaving the padded door open behind him. He chattered as he trotted around the table, glancing at the legal pads as if looking for a place card. "Well, anybody know? How about you two?" He poked an accusing finger at Boyle and Bradley.

"Excuse me," Boyle murmured, and sidled as far from the newcomer as he could. That was only six feet—the wall stopped him in mid-sidle and he bounced—but it looked farther. By some trick of perspective he seemed to shrink and disappear into the distance.

"Paulie Klein," the newcomer said. "I couldn't make it this morning, just plain overslept. Anybody call roll or anything?" He peered around and past people, strained to reach tiptoe but that wasn't much help since he stood a scant five-five, even in the stack-heeled Tony Lama ostrich-skin boots he wore. When only murmurs and the sight of barbered napes answered him, he looked at Mike. "Well?"

"Mike Bradley."

"Okay if I sit here?" Klein dragged a chair back from the table and dropped into it. "About two-thirds of the way down the table's best. That way the big guy"—his waving thumb indicated the head chair—"can see you without really hearing what you say. Too close to him, and he never sees you. Too far away, and he thinks you don't care. Do you care?"

Smiling, Mike sat down beside him. "Not since this morning."

"Good. That's the way to survive this crap. Hang loose. I ought to know. It's my fourth training program this year. Surprise you, huh? There was this brokerage house in New York, only they got mad when I couldn't pronounce debent . . . deebeen . . . something technical. Then a bank up the street here. And General Motors, till they kicked me out for wearing my uncle's Ralph Nader button. They're all the same, these big operations. Hang loose, is what I say."

Mike felt the other trainees staring at Klein as if he were their poor relative. At close range Paulie reminded him of a St. Bernard pup, all noise and clumsy paws. He slid his chair closer. "Four in a year? That's got to be some kind of record."

Paulie grinned at the dozen men staring at him, as if they were his rich relatives. "That's not it. Y'see, all these big places they like to kind of balance out the group. First they hire a couple women, maybe one or two blacks, then a token liberal, one Jew, maybe even a hippie retread, y'know? Now me, in these clothes, I'm three of the five, as far as they're concerned—liberal, Jew, dressed funny. Saves them a ton, one check instead of three. They take me on, they feel better, I sit and collect my check for the training week."

"But don't you finish the program?"

"Oh, sure, but then there's no permanent opening ever turns up for me. I hang in there till they take the class picture. Then, *pfffft!* Downsize, starting with me." He leaned closer. "That's really the way I like it. I pick up spending money this way, it gets me out of the house, and I'm only treading water till I hit it big in my own line." He flopped the sketchpad to the polished tabletop. "I design wallpaper. Freelance."

Mike pondered for a moment but thought of nothing to say.

"I know. It always stumps people. They think, 'wallpaper, hmmm? What's to say about wallpaper?' One thing I can tell you, those damn vinyls are cutting my throat! Prices so high, half your contractors are switching to paint." Paulie slumped in depression and flipped open his sketchpad.

On it, Mike saw only colored squiggles. A question mark mating with a worm. Lethargic spaghetti. Cheerios and shoestrings. He watched Paulie lick the tip of an orange pencil, circle the end of one worm, and push the pad out to arm's length to admire his work.

Across the table from Mike, the man named Boyle pontificated. He aimed a delicate finger at one trainee and said, "Princeton, am I right?"

"How could you tell?"

"Partly the pinstripe, and your brown shoes with that gray suit. I might have said Harvard, but your shoes aren't loafers, and your speech lacks that Kennedy contamination. Now your friend there beside you, I'd say he's . . . oh, Big Ten, somewhere."

A square-jawed hulk in gabardine nodded. "You got me," he said. "Ohio State. What tipped it off?"

Boyle said, "The generic haircut and the accent, that Midwestern twang you've got. Oh"—he was apologetic—"I don't find it as offensive as most people would, but it is rather thick."

Paulie Klein interrupted, grinning. "Hey! That's really cool. Let me take a shot at it."

"I don't think we've got anyone else here from Brandeis or Yeshiva, Klein," Boyle said.

Mike felt Paulie flinch. Now he knew why he didn't like Boyle. "Don't be selfish," he said. "It seems like an easy game. I'd say you went to Williams."

Boyle shrugged. "So?"

Enthralled, Ohio State asked, "How'd you know that?"

"A minute ago I saw Boyle's class ring," Mike said, "when he was picking his nose."

Paulie choked and lowered his head, chuckling. Boyle pushed back from the table and took his clenched jaw to the other end of the room.

"Never mind, Mike," Klein said. "Those guys just roll off my knife."

"Maybe so, but—"

"Hey! See the looker coming in?" Paulie pointed at the door leading to the hallway.

A statuesque black woman six feet tall in her heels and made taller by the bushy corona of her natural hairdo strode into the room carrying a sequin-encrusted attaché case, dressed in a vested tweed suit, man's shirt, and necktie.

"Esther! How are you?" Klein jumped up to greet her.

"Just making it, Paulie. Buck-a-day."

"Esther Flett, this is Mike Bradley. I was telling him about the soft touch I got."

"And Paulie doesn't know the half of it." She brushed Mike's raised palm. "These days a black woman can go places they'd check the pope's ID. Forget whether I can do the job or not, they want me here to punch up their workforce numbers, same as Paulie."

"Doesn't it get to you? The reason they hire you, I mean?"

Esther smiled. "Hey, I'm flavor of the month, that's all. I know this one dude, a blind Puerto Rican, he's got a part-time job right now, wearing a tie and sitting in some bank window. Twenty bucks an hour, and it beats the hell out of washing dishes."

"Hey, sit, sit," Paulie whispered, tugging a chair close for her.

At the head of the room were a bow tie and a Cheshire smile gleaming in the doorway. They entered, on the bulbous waddling hulk of Carleton Weiss, B.A., M.B.A., Ph.D. (Psychology), and Million-A-Year Club member. Their training leader, Weiss had drunk a four-martini lunch. He tumbled olive pits in one hand like a corporate Captain Queeg.

"Heigh-ho!" Weiss sang out.

The room was quiet.

"Once more, now. Heigh-ho!"

Sixteen mouths opened. Nine voices said, "Heigh-ho!"

"That's the spirit! Way to go!" Weiss beamed at them and began to wobble a path around the table like a sailor on a rolling deck. "It's a great idea. From now on we start all our sessions with a little lung exercise. It sets the blood moving to the brain, makes us all raring to go, right?"

"Right!" Louder this time, led by popeyed Boyle, whose corded neck swelled with effort.

"Good-oh. Afraid I was a teensy bit formal there this morning. But if we're going to spend the next week together, better loosen up, I always say. Later I'll divide you into teams for some competition—Auto, Life, Group Health, and so on. But for now, we're all working together with one aim in mind. We're going to make this the best damn training class old Heritage ever had. Am I right?"

"RIGHT!"

"Sweet Jesus," Mike said.

Paulie Klein drew a green worm.

"Now let me hear from you—name, rank, serial number, so to speak." Weiss lumbered around the circle, swiveling heads following him, till he reached his own vacant chair. He dropped into it and sat with dewlaps swaying. His forefinger pointed at Boyle, nearest on his left. "Go!"

Boyle popped erect like hot toast. "Robert Boyle. I was graduated from Williams this past . . ."

Mike tuned him out and slumped in his chair. To his right, Esther and Paulie were playing tic-tac-toe on the sketchpad, orange Xs, blue Os. He pictured a long week ahead. "I like to help people," he muttered. It sounded no less hollow than it had on Friday.

"Because I said so," George Zordich told the manager at the Camden Heights Earl Sheib outlet. "You paint cars. I got a car I want painted. End of story."

"But look, Mister. Not a mark on it! It's new, and red, and you want it painted what?"

"Beige."

"Beige?"

"That's kind of a creamy tan," the moving van driver chimed in, then backed away from the glare George threw him.

George checked his watch again, fidgeting. "And I'm in a hurry," he said. "I want it done before dark."

"Well I don't know..."

"Listen, dumbass! Lester wants it done, if you ever expect to see any more work from us."

It would be done.

Some insurance companies ask prospective sales agents to complete a correspondence course. Successful applicants, the ones who buy policies for themselves, or sell one to their mother, are handed rate sheets and pointed toward the nearest housing tract to go forth and plan estates. But executives at Heritage were determined that their company would be different. Quality was the object (the five men nearest the top of Heritage called it "class," proving how little they understood the term). And so Weiss had been hired to conduct a week's formal session for would-be salespersons (termed "management trainees" by those same five executives). Every detail about Heritage was contrived to give the best appearance. Good taste, "class" (again), and visible stuffiness were important, because Heritage Old-Line Fidelity Insurance was wholly owned and operated by The Company.

In books, in tales told over doughnuts by idling cops, in cities other than Philadelphia, there are other terms for the founders of Heritage. They're called the syndicate, or the mob, but in the City of Brotherly Love they're The Company—not to be confused with the CIA, a less efficient organization sometimes also called The Company.

Heritage Old-Line Fidelity Insurance is a money laundry. Income from numbers banks, off-track books, drugs hard and soft, girls sweet and low—all of it funnels into Heritage and other businesses like it, mixes with a small dribble of honest income, and rises to the top as cream for the executive staff to skim.

President and Founder of Heritage, and of sixteen other legitimate businesses in town, was Theodore Winthrop (born, reared, and in his youth nine times arrested but never convicted under his real name, Pietro Aiello). Even a Philadelphia cop with balls enough to arrest "Pietro Aiello" would shrink from questioning Main Line–named Theodore Winthrop. Only five men at Heritage knew their president's real name and connections. Carleton Weiss was not one of the five.

Weiss led his charges through actuarial tables and programmed self-deception for the entire afternoon. By 4:00 PM many of the trainees had begun to feel like missionaries whose function in life was to save the improvident masses from their spendthrift habits, to ease the burden of the infirm, to prepare a future for any common man in need of financial counseling. By 4:00 PM Esther Flett had Paulie Klein down eight games to none (sixty-three ties), the tic-tac-toe match had shifted to green and red pencils, and Mike and Paulie had begun a whispered friendship.

"You mean they grabbed your car?" Paulie said.

Under his breath, Mike summarized the scene. He frowned at the grin stretching Paulie's cherubic cheeks. "Why is that funny?"

"We'll get it back."

"You heard Weiss and his statistics. Ninety percent of the cars ripped off in Philadelphia just disappear."

Paulie paid Esther her eight cents and closed his sketchpad. He began a whispered recital of his own in the voice of experience. Mike had worked at no jobs in twenty-four years. In his twenty-six, Paulie had passed through dozens of employers, and among the jobs recorded in his cluttered past—besides shucking clams at Bookbinders, playing kazoo in a street theater company, selling soft pretzels in Fishtown and salt-water taffy in Atlantic City—was a three-month stint forging titles and running a printing press for Lester-the-thief.

"Who the hell's Lester-the-thief?"

"Shhhh!" Near the head of the table Boyle shook his head.

"A guy I know. People go to him with hot cars, he gives them clean papers. When I worked for him he had two trucks kind of like that gray moving van. You order a car from Lester-the-thief, he picks up what you want, paints it, changes the engine number, prints a new title, the works. What economists call a 'vertical trust.' Now, I make it somebody asks Lester for a new Honda Prelude, so he sends a crew out to cop one, is all."

"You're still smiling. Knowing who's got my car doesn't get it back."

"Sure it does. We ask Lester, he gives it back. If the buyer hasn't picked it up yet. He owes me a favor from before, so I'll call him, and he'll give it back. Lester-the-thief's no crook."

Mike doubted both the story and the likelihood of recovering the car. "Look," he whispered. "Why don't I just report it to the cops?"

Paulie's eyebrows rose. "Why would you want to get Lester-the-thief's tit in a wringer?" He winced and turned to Esther Flett. "Sorry."

She shrugged. "Tail in a crack," she said.

"Have you two got something to contribute?" Weiss stood and pointed at them. "What's the discussion?"

Mike watched an instant change sweep over Paulie—embarrassed, tongue-tied, no longer the cocky hustler he'd been a second before. And glancing around the room Mike understood that change. Here, Paulie Klein was out of his element. This wasn't the street, and Paulie didn't know the rules.

"No sir," Mike said, waving Esther quiet. "Sorry if we were making too much noise, but we were talking about how much there is to learn. I guess I never really knew before. There must be lots of experienced insurance men who can't put across what they know."

"Well, I'll admit there's a knack to it." Weiss tried not to smile. He failed. "Let me tell you about the time I watched some over educated economics professor botch up explaining simple annuities." He maundered off in a cloud of self-glorification.

Mike breathed easier and settled back in his chair, while Paulie stared at him with frank admiration.

Esther Fleet leaned past Paulie to whisper, "You got the makings, man. Silver tongue, like they say. Only see if I go down a dark road with you anytime soon."

Mike and Paulie planned their appeal to Lester-the-thief.

"He's back." Harry Schaeffer sat beside a third floor window overlooking Pine Street. Across the way other four-story row houses converted to apartments faced him. In the street below, Mike Bradley and Paulie Klein stood near the stoop, talking. Harry pushed the earplug of his transistor radio deeper into his ear and doodled on a tablet. "And I think he's in trouble."

Harry's daughter Lee was busy at her loom in the dark, room-and-a-half apartment. Her eye had just found a mistake four rows back in the pattern she was working out, and she debated changing the pattern to incorporate the error. Either that, or ravel and reweave for ten minutes. Weaving was half a hobby, half a job for Lee. She had sold a few pieces of her handiwork at a head shop on South Street, and what she couldn't sell was hung, draped, thrown, or piled somewhere in the apartment. It was economical, she claimed. They didn't need to buy rugs or drapes.

"Bad plan," Harry always said. "You sell any good piece you make, we get to live with the rejects."

"Want to move out?" she asked.

Harry coughed and went back to his hobby. His didn't pay. He listened to Talk Radio. He had a fine ear for nuances of dialect and accents, the convolutions of syntax, and he kept track of telephoning regulars on a ruled pad beside him. Some of the regulars called in with comments every day. Harry knew who, and when. "Nothing better to do with their time," he often said. Written out in fine script on inner sheets of the tablet were Harry's witty rejoinders to their expressed opinions. He might have phoned the station to read his retorts aloud—he often threatened to do just that—but by the time he composed an answer clever enough to share, the conversation had shifted to another topic. Harry Schaeffer lived at his own pace, one argument behind the world.

He wore a Chinese dressing gown and rabbit-fur mukluks, but even that swaddling didn't protect him from the drafts he felt, and every few minutes complained about. A reluctant sixty, exhausted-looking, balding, Harry enjoyed vigorous good health. He had been ill only once in his life, an attack of hypochondria lasting sixty years. He summed his problems in a single phrase used to greet all strangers. In answer to "How do you do?" Harry always said, "Allergict. I'm allergict." It gave him privacy, and—he thought—a touch of mystery: he didn't know what he was allergic to. No one with good sense asked, because even the most insincere polite question opened the floodgates holding back a litany of Harry's ailments. VA doctors knew better than to ask; Harry's practiced hacking cough was persuasive enough to satisfy them when they reviewed his case, and the disability checks kept on coming.

His daughter Lee looked as healthy as Harry actually was. She shone, a quality that made privacy infrequent. She was mistaken for an actress by people who didn't know that all actresses have acne and an overbite. She hated her own shining good looks. Plain, she might have escaped attention. Everyone who entered her life somehow changed it, and she wanted nothing more than the status quo. No changes, no threats to her peace and security, nothing about tomorrow different from today. She envied plain people, but nature had made her the way she was.

And the way she was—especially her bewildering vegetarianism—amazed her father Harry, who longed to munch his way to artery-hardened old age on Jimmy Dean sausage and cheese sandwiches. But everything Lee prepared for them started its vegetable life green in color and lost most fat and all flavor on its way to his plate. Mike loved her enough to endure and pretend to enjoy the endless salads. Harry loved her too but said to anyone who would listen, "How the hell she can be my daughter I'll never know. I'd suspect her Ma of playing around on me, except that woman never could shut up for the time it would take."

He stared at her now in petulance. "You're not listening to me again."

"I'm sorry, Daddy. What did you say? Mike's in 'trouble'?"

"Shhh." Harry pressed his earplug tighter. "It's that old lady from the Main Line, talking about drugs."

Lee pushed her stool back from the loom and crossed to him. She pulled his earplug loose and turned off the radio. "Why did you say 'trouble'?"

"Hey! How'm I gonna hear—"

"Daddy? Look at me."

"Oh, see for yourself." He pointed out the window at Mike and Paulie. "Twice now in the last four days he's worn my suit, and there's some hippie with him. It's trouble, all right."

They watched Mike and Paulie part, then listened to his footsteps pounding up the stairs. Mike scratched at the door. "Lee? It's me."

She slipped the chain to let him in.

"I don't think you're going to like this," Mike began.

"What did I say?" Harry plugged in again and turned away from them. He had a delicate sense of propriety and tried not to watch their lovers' quarrels. When there was something good on the radio.

Mike started over, a lame explanation that got no further than his first confession.

"That's why the suit!" Lee said. She backed him away with the vehemence of her accusation. "You got a job!"

"Well.... Not a real job. I just—"

"After all you promised, you went out and got a job." She squeezed her eyes shut and tried to draw tears. When anger didn't work with Mike, crying did.

"Working's not contagious; Harry won't catch it. And knock off the phony crying." Mike threw up his hands in disgust and walked to toss his tie over a chair back. "How about that?" he asked no one in particular. "A guy gets a simple little job and it comes out sounding like leprosy. People all over the world have jobs, but I'm supposed to—"

"You promised! How many times have we talked about it? You'll meet new people, everything will change. Remember?"

Mike put his arm around her stiff shoulders. "Look, Babe. It's only a training program. One week. Chances are I'll quit before it's done. And even if I stay, who am I going to meet in a mausoleum like that? A place like an insurance company, it's so stuffy and dull you never meet anybody. Trust me. Have I ever let you down? I can take care of you. We—"

"It's the principle of the thing."

"We've got to pay the rent, buy food—"

"We're doing fine the way things are now."

"—make the car payments, so forth, so on...." Sneak it past her like that, maybe she wouldn't notice.

She noticed. "What car payments?" She backed away a step and stared at him. "What did you do?"

"A married couple should have a car. That's the other thing: will you marry me?"

"Only if you're pregnant."

"It's time we got married. I know how you—"

"You've flipped out! And don't think you can finesse this 'car payment' thing."

"Well . . . I guess I should explain. Come here." He took her arm and pulled her into the alcove they called their bedroom. "Harry will hear you."

"Not till the station break. Now what's this about a car?"

"How do you think it feels, living with your father?"

"I live with him too."

"No. He lives with us! A guy's got some pride, right?"

"Not Daddy, and don't change the—"

"I meant me! I've got pride and—"

"Not too proud to go to work, I can see that." Lee sniffed and bit her lip. Damn! The tears just wouldn't come. "I ought to move out."

"Will you take Harry with you?"

"Leave Daddy out of this. It's his disability check that pays—"

"Mike?" Harry stood in the curtained archway. "Mind taking off the pants?"

"The pants?"

"It's my good suit. If you're moving out—"

"Daddy, get out of here."

Harry pulled his robe tight around his neck and shuffled away. Coughing. Martyred, he turned to face them. "*Harrgh, harrgh.* Ahh, see? That's the thanks I get. You know I'm not well, and . . . " His eyes glazed and he felt for the pencil in the pocket of his robe.

"Go ahead, say it," Mike told him.

"Shhh!" Harry poked his earplug in tighter. "It's the wop with the lisp. Third time this week he's called in." He dashed for his tablet.

Lee said, "Now, what's this about a car?'

Mike hopped on one foot, half in, half out of Harry Schaeffer's pants. It was not a good homecoming. And he still hadn't explained about Lester-the-thief.

At 8:15 that night Paulie Klein picked them up in a four-year-old VW. "I borrowed it from a friend," he told Lee, after Mike had introduced them. He couldn't stop smiling at her.

She sat in the other front bucket seat, nibbling from a baggie full of cold, boiled lima beans (and an occasional white grape for surprise), while Mike hunched crossways in the back, his long legs stretched out seeking comfort. "You're sure about this Lester giving the car back?" she asked.

"Wait and see. We won't do any worse there than we did with the cops. Tell her, Mike."

Mike shook his head. "Go ahead. You were the one who enjoyed it." He sat and endured Paulie's summary.

It was accurate enough. The two of them had gone straight to the police station from the Heritage Building. After a twenty-minute wait they were ushered into a cubicle where an off-duty meter maid filled out enough forms to found a government. They were not reassured when she moved her lips as she drew the letters. After completing the forms, she promised to mail notification to the state capitol at Harrisburg, "and we'll put your car in next week's list." She even showed them a sample list that all prowl cars carried, clipped to the visor above the driver's head.

"License numbers," Paulie said. A constant giggle cluttered his speech. "Here was this sheet of paper maybe a foot long, with nothing on it but three columns of license numbers, no car descriptions, nothing. Nobody cares about one stolen car. Cops are out hunting for stolen license plates, right Mike?"

"Right, right. Now watch where you're driving."

"So Mike asks her, 'what happens if the thief changes plates on the car?' And she's got to admit, 'then we probably won't get it back.' So that's when I phone Lester-the-thief."

"A new car." Lee's voice was sad and wondering.

Mike avoided her gaze as she turned to look at him. He studied instead the lights on the river below as the VW swung up and over the Ben Franklin Bridge, headed for New Jersey. Traffic was sparse, rush hour over now, and only two lanes were open in each direction. He could feel Lee's stare, but even more he could feel his own irritation at the meter maid's unconcern. If they could get the car back from Lester-the-thief, he would report having found it abandoned somewhere and let it go at that. He still wasn't certain why he'd asked Lee to accompany them tonight, but even that didn't matter too much. His ego was bruised: in the Heritage conference room, Paulie had been uncomfortable and out of his element. Here, on their way to visit Lester-the-thief, it was Mike who had to take the backseat. Literally and figuratively. He didn't like the feeling.

To top it, Lee spent the first five minutes in the car debating aloud how someone as clever as she'd always considered Mike to be could lose a new car. Nothing he told her about the thieves' efficiency impressed her. The episode made her disappointed in him. In some indefinable way he had failed her, she admitted with grave reluctance, in response to no question at all. Out of her bountiful good nature she forgave him, she said. She forgave him. Over and over. She forgave him.

Paulie pulled into a vacant lane approaching one of the tollbooths and passed three dollars through the open window. "Hey, mister, I've been wondering. Does this buy our way into New Jersey, or out of Philadelphia?"

"Trucks only, kid," the uniformed attendant told him. "Cars pay heading west. Into New Jersey's free. Coming back into Philadelphia will cost you three bucks."

"Is that a buck each person or three bucks for the car?"

The attendant shook his head. "Don't try to figure it, kid. If the light's red, three bucks turns the light green, okay?"

Paulie laughed and pulled away. "There's a mind-blowing job for you, Mike, standing there all night making change."

"What? Sorry, I wasn't listening."

"No, he was calculating a day's take on that gate, weren't you?" Lee turned to smile at him in the strobe-like flickering of streetlights stuttering past. "Have a bean."

Mike wasn't listening. "If you figure eight lanes, with an average of—"

"That's my man. A brand-new car gone, and he's still the same guy." Lee turned to Paulie. "What do you think?"

"I don't like cold beans."

"No—about Mike."

"I think you should forgive him."

Mike sat back and let the pair comfortable in the front bucket seats laugh at him. Calculating the take on the bridge was easy. A greater part of his preoccupation centered on Lester-the-thief. That modified moving van was intriguing, with its hoist and counterweights. Anyone who could devise something so simple yet so effective had an interesting mind; Lester sounded like someone not to play poker with. Paulie had assured Mike that the meeting involved no danger—a small misunderstanding between friends, easy to clear up. Lester-the-thief owed Paulie a favor, details unspecified, and Paulie was making his claim. As simple as that.

"Maybe half an hour and we'll be there," Paulie said.

They watched Camden's neon-lit streets become a highway threading through suburbs dotted with junkyards and high-rise apartments. The traffic thinned to a few carloads of kids helling from one bar to another and semi-trailers headed for Philadelphia carrying produce, furniture, anything.

They passed through Cherry Hill and a string of motels, along sand-scrub bordered roads, past an abandoned quarry, Mike rehearsing conversations and trying to picture Lester-the-thief, while Lee and Paulie chatted about nothing.

At a two-pump country service station on the edge of the Jersey pine barrens, Paulie swung off the highway onto a dirt road. An old man in bib overalls sat tilted back on a camp chair beside the gasoline pumps and tried not to notice their arrival. The VW slid to a stop in a shower of dust and gravel that made his nonchalance difficult to sustain, but he carried it off.

Paulie rolled down his window. "Hey! Can we get some service?"

"Delivery didn't come in," the man recited. "Pumps are dry." Stolid, he sat immobile in his chair and spoke without moving his lips. He might have been a mummy.

"I don't want gas. How about a grease job?"

"We charge a lot for that." Still no movement.

Paulie switched on the overhead light and held a slip of paper near it, then stuck his head out the window again. "Do you charge more than Aunt Mary?"

The man leapt off his chair and startled all of them. Including himself. He stood bug-eyed as if amazed to find himself standing.

"Aunt Mary?" Mike asked.

Paulie shrugged. "That's what it says." He reached back to hand Mike a slip of paper covered with a clutter of cryptic abbreviations. "Nobody gets in without the password, and that's it for today."

"Let me see that." The attendant reached in the window to snatch the paper from Mike's hand. He walked around the VW, examining it, ran his forefinger inside the tailpipe, kicked a tire twice, then shrugged. "Follow me." He strolled toward the corner of the station, with Paulie inching along behind in low gear.

They lurched off the gravel drive over a grassy hump and bounced down a pair of deep ruts toward a broken-spined, three-story barn sagging toward them. Paulie kept the ridge of the car's hood sighted on the man's back and mouthed a machine gun's chatter.

"In there." The man waved them into the barn and stepped aside, into darkness.

"Where'd he go?" Lee asked.

"Still sure you want to come along?" Mike reached over the seat back to rub her shoulders. "You could wait here."

"I'll stay with you." She slid forward to let her seat tilt.

Mike struggled out of the car past Lee, pulled the huge barn door aside. The VW's headlights showed them an open doorway at the other end of the barn and, beyond it, a rutted path. After closing the door behind them, Mike clambered back into the car. "Is your friend always so cautious? What's all this stuff about a password?"

"Lester-the-thief is methodical, is all. It's not like you want just anyone barging in here."

"I don't want us barging in here, but here we are."

"Don't worry about me," Lee said. "I want two minutes to tell this Lester what I think of his ripping off our new car, then—"

"Hey now!" Paulie slipped the car into neutral and turned to face her. "You didn't bring a weapon or something dumb like that, did you?"

"Did you say 'our' car?" Mike asked.

She nodded and said to Paulie, "No weapon."

"Okay, but no trouble. Lester-the-thief is a nice guy and all, but he doesn't like being contradicted, if you know what I mean. And for sure not on his own turf. These pine barrens are big and empty."

"What's that mean?" Lee said. "Jimmy Hoffa–land?"

Only after Lee promised to let Paulie do the talking did the VW inch forward again, through the towering empty barn and out the doorless side. A sign greeted them: "LIGHTS?" And past that, another read: "SEAT BELTS?"

"Seat belts?" Lee asked.

"I make it Lester-the-thief's got a friend in the highway department. You know those signs you see when you come out of the turnpike tunnels? He probably picked up a couple of them somewhere. He's real thrifty that way."

He was also, they discovered, more than cautious. Driving along a path through the pine woods they were twice more stopped by men sitting on camp chairs astride the grassy hump that separated deep tire ruts. Both times they passed a test by claiming to know Aunt Mary.

"He's not 'cautious,'" Mike said. "He's paranoid. What's the sense of posting three sentries? How would we get this far without passing that first one inside that barn?"

"All I know is, Lester's never been busted, so 'cautious' does him some good," Paulie said. "Maybe those guys are relatives. There's always a lot of people on the payroll, is all I know. Even me once, remember?"

"Let's hope Lester remembers," Lee said.

The VW lurched over a small knoll into a clearing among the pines. Six cars sat parked on a gravel lot bordered on three sides by galvanized Quonset huts, only the hut opposite their entrance lighted at the moment. The light dimmed as two silhouettes filled the narrow doorway.

Paulie said, "That's him."

"He," Lee corrected.

"Lester?" Mike asked

"And his man George with him." Paul stopped the car and got out, pointing. "The big guy." He ducked under a cloud of mosquitoes and moths that surrounded the VW and flitted through the hood louvers to hit the hot engine block with the sizzle of their suicides.

A swath of light swept over the white gravel as the two men unblocked the Quonset hut doorway. George sprayed a path of Raid through the air ahead of them. Lester-the-thief trailed along, choking.

"Who's there?"

"Lester? It's me, Paulie Klein. I brought the guy I called you about." He waved Mike forward into the cloud of Raid. "Mike, meet Lester."

The light behind Lester hid his features. Mike had time only to sense wiry smallness before he met a crushing handshake that tested his. He leaned against Lester's tensed grip for a moment till the pressure relaxed.

"Now you trust me, right?"

Mike shook his sore fingers. "If nothing's broken."

Lester-the-thief laughed. "Me too. All that macho crap. Only you'd be surprised how many people get faked out by a handshake." He turned away. "Come in where we can see," he said over his shoulder. "Bring the girl along, if you want. She's a pretty one."

"I'm not a 'girl,'" Lee muttered.

"Then you're one hell of a pretty boy."

"Come on." Paulie danced ahead, beckoning them through the spray-moistened air.

They stood blinking in the bright room. Mike watched Lester dismiss the Raid-bearer with a lofty wave and stalk to a kidney-shaped mahogany desk atop a low platform two-thirds of the way down the long hut. Beyond the desk were two doors labeled "Camille" and "Lucille."

Lester wore wheat-colored jeans, silver sandals, and a kelly green shirt unbuttoned rock-star-deep down his chest to display a silver Navajo medallion. He pranced more than walked, a lightweight boxer or a pacing horse, taut muscle and sinew, built for speed.

Lester's bodyguard, George Zordich, sat in a camp chair near the door and clasped his hands in his lap like a well-behaved nursery schooler. His bulk made the pose seem contrived.

"Gimme a sec," Lester said. He shuffled through papers atop his desk.

"We didn't come here to wait all night," Lee said.

"Shhhh!" Paulie Klein shook his head and waved a calming hand toward the bodyguard.

"Oh, for God's sake!" Lee folded her arms and examined the room.

Along the left wall stood a dozen straight-backed chairs; across from them, on the right, five more, a Coke cooler, two women in their fifties seated on a cracked black leather couch, and a third in a platform rocker. The pair on the couch, dressed in identical pink-and-white pinafores and checked hair ribbons, were grotesque, painted twins, trying to look twenty but failing by two generations. The third woman was old—parchment complexion, Supp-Hose, ballet slippers worn through at the toe, and a coin changer cinched around her waist, hidden, then revealed, by the sag of her pendulous bosom as she rocked back and forth. Beside her stood a gaudy Wurlitzer jukebox bubbling a multi-colored rainbow through the glass tubes topping it.

The old woman stood to meet them. "Want a beer?"

"Sure," Paulie said.

Mike and Lee shook their heads and watched Lester-the-thief, busy with papers at his desk and ignoring them.

"Rolling Rock," the woman said, taking a sweating can from the Coke cooler. "One buck."

"My treat." Lester didn't look up, even when the woman walked over to accept four quarters from him and slip them into her coin changer. "Be with you in a minute," he said. "Dance with the girls, if you want. Meet Camille and Lucille."

The twins tittered and stood up to be examined. "Buck a dance," Camille said, in a voice full of rusty tin cans. "Or buy me a beer."

Mike glanced at "the girls," but spoke to Lester. "Your treat?"

Lucille answered. "You can pay Ma."

"Another time." Mike turned to Lee, who in turn turned her back and stood with arms folded, staring into the darkness through a screened window. He didn't like her tensed posture. It meant trouble—for all of them now, or for him later.

They waited, standing another three minutes, till Lester slammed down his pencil and beckoned. "Okay. Let's get this settled."

Paulie trotted to the platform and summarized the situation, at times looking to Mike for nodded confirmation.

"Got a license number?" Lester asked.

Mike handed over his temporary registration.

Lester studied it for a moment. From a desk drawer he took out a few papers, slipped them into an envelope and handed them to Mike. "It's all yours."

"Again," Lee said.

"Miss? You know the saying, 'pretty is as pretty does'?"

"I know you like hearing yourself—"

"Paulie, keep her quiet. I said, the Honda's all yours . . . as soon as you pay expenses. Let's say, two-oh-one-ninety-five."

Lee exploded. "Of all the . . . Two hundred dollars, for our own car? How can you—"

"Take her out of here."

George rose from his chair.

"I don't think so," Mike said, stepping between them. It seemed expected of him.

George smiled at the idea and looked to Lester, who shook his head. "Fine. Let her stay, if you want, but you've got to tell me these things. I can't work in the dark." He held out a ledger book to show Mike. "Let me explain. I've got expenses like any other businessman. Because you're a friend of Paulie's, we'll let some slide." His pencil point ticked off items: "New registration, new block and frame numbers, skip 'em. I'll eat the cost."

Mike was dazzled. "You got all that done since noon?"

Lester-the-thief didn't bother to hide his pleased smile. "Now the paint job, that's another—"

"You painted it, too?"

"Picked it up less than an hour ago, from Earl Scheib," Lester admitted. "Those guys work faster and cheaper than I can do it, and their bill comes off my taxes."

"Your taxes," Lee repeated with withering scorn.

Lester didn't look Lee's way but said to Mike, "In just about a minute I'm going to rap her in the mouth. Now, I run a business here, supply a service—'Cars to Order.' I run it clean, don't screw around with The Company big guys, never cross a state line, unless I have to. I pay taxes like anybody else. You think I want trouble? The paint job, I said, and couple bucks for gas. You take it or leave it."

Lee sighed and walked over to stare at the jukebox.

"Fair's fair," Paulie whispered, and Mike reached for his wallet.

"You'll like it," Lester promised. "Red's too gaudy, you know? It's a nice quiet beige, now. That color alone's worth a couple hundred at trade-in. Unique. You got the only beige Honda Prelude in the world." He took the money, counted it twice, gave Mike a nickel change from a desk drawer. "Let's get the car. You two wait here." He and Mike left.

When they returned a few minutes later, Mike was arguing with soft vehemence, Lester shaking his head in a superior way.

"Don't teach me to suck eggs, kid. That junkyard dodge is old stuff. You been watching too much TV."

Crestfallen, Mike lagged a step behind.

"Tell him, Paulie. Where do I get clean titles?"

"Besides printing them, there's . . . Oh, you mean the wrecks? Well, y'see Mike, if Lester has, say a new Buick, say like an oh-four, he goes to a junkyard to find a wreck of the same model. The he switches engine numbers on the two cars—"

"He told me." Mike didn't like the feeling of defeat and liked even less the disappointed look Lee wore. On top of his stupidity in losing the Honda, in having to pay to get it back, he was talking his way into more embarrassment. Mike Bradley, hustler first-class, being shown up by a skinny crook called Lester. He didn't like the feeling at all.

Lester laughed. "Amateurs! After twenty years in the business, I don't guess there's a trick I don't know."

Paulie jumped in, half to rescue Mike from his embarrassment and half to forestall the torrent he could sense building in Lee. He said, "Did you ever get a rig big enough to boost Lincolns?"

Lester's smile disappeared. "Okay, Paulie, drop it. There's no real market in those."

"Or Cadillacs? I remember you couldn't pick up a Caddy or the big Lincoln with your trucks." Paulie turned to Mike. "I hear George he tried it once, got a Caddy on the forklift, tipped the front wheels of the moving van right up off the street. It must have—"

"Paulie?" George rumbled closer. "Don't start up, man. I'll have to punch you out."

"Me? What am I starting? Only"—to Lester—"I remember a time when you could sell an El Dorado a day, except nobody was bringing them in."

Lester nodded. "Still true, in a way. I'd pay two, maybe three K for any new Caddy that showed up tonight."

"And sell it for ten."

"Twelve-five." Lester smiled at the thought but grew stern again. "Knock it off! I've got work to do. And you girls. . . ." The twins snapped to attention. "If there's nobody in by ten thirty, you can pack it in."

"Sure, Lester."

"Monday's a drag, anyhow."

Mike nudged Paulie. "Dance with one of them, will you? I want to talk to Lester a minute."

Lee's eyes flashed warnings. "Mike? Don't start something new. I went along with you this far, but you're pushing now. Leave well enough alone."

"Five minutes, that's all." He faced Lester's curious expression. "What would you give for a Cadillac with a clean title?"

"Still brainstorming, kid?" He snickered. "Okay, we'll talk, but I'm telling you, you're in over your head."

Lee tugged at Mike's sleeve. "Just what do I do while you're talking?"

"Make plans, Babe, to spend a little windfall coming our way." He followed Lester-the-thief toward the large desk.

Lester winked at her. "Dance with the other one, Honey."

The twins were both offended. Camille said, "I don't dance with no women." She flounced back to her leather couch and sat sulking. Lee stood beside the jukebox grinding her teeth, while Paulie steered Lucille tittering around the dance floor through a pair of polkas. Only when "Moonglow" drifted from the Wurlitzer did he lose his nerve and abandon Lucille to her mother. And paid. Two dances, two dollars.

Mike talked. Lester-the-thief listened, shrugged, nodded, and Mike jumped down off the platform. "Let's go," he said.

"One thing first." Paulie beckoned Lester to the doorway. "What's that VW worth to you? The one I drove in?"

Lee asked, "The one you borrowed from a friend?"

"You caught on, huh? I didn't want to make you nervous, is all. I hot-wired it on Locust a couple blocks from your place." He looked at Lester. "Well?"

Lester glanced outside in perfunctory ritual, then took a green princess phone off its cradle beside the door and pressed one of three buttons. "Jack? Did you get a good look at the VW you let in? . . . Uh-huh. Uh-huh. . . . Paulie Klein. . . . Uh-huh. I think so."

He replaced the receiver and tapped a tooth with his thumbnail before speaking. "Three-fifty," he said.

"Hey, Lester! This is me, Paulie Klein! I know better. Three hundred fifty bucks for a clean Beetle is—"

"Three-twenty-five."

"Come on, man! You know the risk I took. If I—"

"Three hundred."

"What the hell kind of bargaining is that?" Paulie stamped his foot and whirled around in frustration. "Do you hear what—"

"Take the three hundred," Mike said. He was watching Lester with great interest, measuring him.

"Listen to your friend, Paulie. He understands quick."

"But he's slow to share what he understands," Lee snapped. She pushed past them and went outside. "I'll be in the car."

"Lee?" Mike went after her.

Grumbling, but not loud enough to cost himself any more money, Paulie watched $300 being counted into his palm. When he joined the others in the mosquito-rich parking lot Lee was already seated in the shallow backseat of a beige Prelude; Mike circled the car, inspecting.

"Here you are," Paulie said. "Two hundred bucks. Now you're even again."

Mike took the money and slid into the driver's seat. He reached across to throw Paulie's door open.

Leaning forward, in a voice dripping honey, Lee said, "Paulie? Will you ask your friend behind the wheel to drive us straight home and keep out of any more trouble?"

Mike glanced in the rearview mirror but said nothing. He shrugged at Paulie's rolled eyes. "We'll see," he said. He didn't know what he meant by that.

He maintained a careful silence as they retraced the dirt track through the pines back to the highway, almost ignoring Lee and Paulie. He played and replayed in imagination the sight of his new Honda rising into the air and floating out of sight inside the truck that would carry it off for a cosmetic makeover. There was something aesthetic about the whole irritating sequence. Something beautiful in the planning as well as in the execution. Who would ever think of picking up an automobile? He loved it!

Mike stopped the car once on the way out of the woods to measure the barn door width by pacing it and stepped back to peer up and estimate its height. His mood lightened. A smile played across his lips.

Before they had crossed the bridge back into Philadelphia the tension in the car diminished. "I'm sorry, Mike, really," Lee said. "We've got the car back, so I guess we're okay... if we really need a car."

"No problem." He kept his eyes on the road and took petty enjoyment in his minor martyrdom, a pettiness that stemmed from guilt: if Lee had lost her temper, the fault was his. She depended on him, and he had let her down, making the kind of stupid mistake Lee would never make. In losing the new Honda that way, he had become something less than they both expected of him. He knew the feeling was only machismo gone sour, but he couldn't do much about it. He apologized.

So did Lee. "I mean it," she persisted. "It's just... oh, I don't know. I don't like seeing you do dumb things." Her laughter was strained.

"Forget it."

"You're sure?"

"As long as you're not mad at me," he said. Then, after a moment: "Was it really so dumb, what I said to Lester?"

Lee hunched forward and tapped Paulie's shoulder. Her eyes begged his help. "I didn't mean *dumb* dumb. I meant... well... That Lester, he's a professional, right Paulie?"

"Right. Professional." He took the cue. "He's like a small independent. He's not tied up with The Company, but with his head he doesn't need them and all their accountants and lawyers. Just plain smart, is what Lester is."

Mike nodded, leading them down the verbal path he was clearing ahead of them. "So if smart Lester-the-thief doesn't know something about stealing cars, it's not worth knowing."

"That's it!" Paulie said, pleased that he'd got it right. "Lee knows. You can't walk in cold and tell a pro like Lester how to do his job."

Nodding, Lee said, "It's only experience, not like he's so smart. There are lots of things Mike knows that Lester doesn't, right Paulie?"

"Like what?" At Mike's look, he changed direction. "Oh, sure, must be lots of things."

"And one of them's how to recognize a good idea when it comes along," Mike said. He let the smug remark hang in silence, unexplained. Pressed for details, he couldn't have been more specific. Not just then. "But the night's not over, either," he said.

Lee bounced close and kissed his ear. "Right! What do we do now?"

"Come to my place!" Paulie clapped his hands with a sharp crack and grew animated. "I've got a gallon jug of dago red and some 'Grandpa Rock,' the Stones' fifth farewell tour."

With Paulie directing they swung off the bridge exit ramp and south along the river to a warehouse near the foot of Washington Avenue. "Stop anywhere along here," he said. "That's it."

Paulie Klein lived in a loft over an echoing, cavernous warehouse. "My old man's," he told them, leading the way through a small side door. "I like it here, he doesn't need to pay a watchman, and we don't have to see each other at breakfast. A good deal for both of us."

"Hello! Hello!" Lee threw echoes into the darkness. "It's empty."

"The old man claims he's keeping it available, in case he gets a buyer. Truth is, we've got so many building violations slapped on the place, only the violations papers hold it together. Now wait right there." Paulie posed them near the doorway and walked off.

They listened to his footsteps fading away, then both flinched at his shout.

"Over here! Watch!" He snapped on overhead lights and with a sweeping bow directed their eyes toward a side wall. Eighty feet wide by twenty high, it was covered with hanging strips of white butcher paper waving in the breeze from the open door. "My samples," he announced.

A few strips showed climbing arbutus or lilies twining their freehand way up the wall; others were more patterned—plaids, stripes, one a series of obelisks mounting in a tiered design like a picket fence. But the greatest number were off-white, only implying color, at least at a distance.

Lee and Mike walked closer to examine the hand-painted paper and watched, with each step they took, white shading to pastel, as small lines, dots, meandering squiggles grew visible with proximity. They were treated to a detailed explanation of Paul Joseph Klein's master plan: he would hold his own one-man show, by invitation only, for buyers from all the major fabric and wallpaper firms in the East.

Still bubbling on, he led them up a flight of rickety wooden steps to the two-room loft he'd furnished with St. Vincent de Paul rejects and Salvation Army reconstruction failures. He broke out his wine, fed a pair of CDs into the changer, and tried his best to involve Mike in a celebration he and Lee feigned for Mike's benefit.

It didn't work. Mike was withdrawn. When one of them asked him a direct question he blinked, smiled, asked them to repeat it, and answered before returning to his preoccupation.

A leaden hour later Lee and Mike drove home. "You're not still mad, are you?" she asked as they climbed to their apartment.

"Just thinking."

Harry sat glassy-eyed, plugged in, tuned in, turned off. But even in the privacy Harry's condition gave them Lee couldn't entice Mike to bed.

"Not for a minute, anyway. You go ahead. I'm working something out."

He sat at their Formica-topped breakfast-cum-dining table, doodling, watching Harry on his cot shake his head in silent sadness at the banality droning through his earplug. Mike's cheeks tingled as if Lester-the-thief had slapped him with a glove—or as if Lee's criticism only now urged a blush to the surface. Either way, he'd been challenged, and sleep was impossible until some means of vindication showed itself. As provocative as the memory of his Honda floating upward into the air might be, he had a new picture in mind. It wasn't clear yet, vague and teasing like an artist's conception. He had to flesh-out and clarify the misty image.

He checked on Lee. She often kidded him about being a "messy" sleeper, sometimes outside the covers, sometimes under the pillow; but that definition was in contrast to her "sleeping neat," she called it. As she was now. Golden hair spread in a halo on the pillow, hands folded outside the covers and centered on her stomach—almost a pose. And wearing the slightest smile. Mike wanted to nestle against her and join in her dream but wanted even more to deserve nestling. He kissed her and went back to the table.

At the top of a sheet of paper he printed "NEW CADILLAC."

Four hours later he crumpled nine note-cluttered pages, satisfied. Lee hadn't moved. Smiling, Mike went to bed. Twenty minutes before the alarm clock woke him.

TUESDAY

"Your four-in-hand's fine. Conservative, reliable... you see a man in a four-in-hand, and you know he's your kind of fellow. But did you ever think about your bow tie? Uhh... you! Klein. Doesn't a bow tie say 'loser' to you?"

Paulie squirmed in the glare of attention and grinned. Weiss waited. They all did, till it became obvious that this question wasn't rhetorical; the man wanted an answer. And Paulie couldn't expect Mike Bradley's help. For the past twenty minutes Mike had slept behind the cupped palm of a hand propped against his eyebrows, elbow on the table, while his other hand held a pencil poised frozen in the midst of taking notes. Faking notes.

"Bow tie, Klein? Bow tie?"

"Well... I never thought much about them, to tell the truth. I always figured anybody who wears one must be some kind of wimp." He saw Weiss' bow tie bobbing like wattles under the man's chins and flinched.

"Exactly!" Weiss beamed and straightened the wings of his bow tie, a gesture imitated by Boyle beside him at the head of the conference table, though Boyle didn't look so pleased at Paulie's jibe. "A wimp. Harmless, is the word. Someone you can dismiss as ineffectual, or unsure of himself. Most of us feel superior to the man in a bow tie, not threatened by him. Take a good look at Boyle here."

That was difficult, since Boyle was tugging at his lower lip, head bowed, chin and starched cuff hiding most of his tie.

"He wore that silly-looking thing today because I had one on yesterday. But I wear mine to make a point. People go by appearances. If you don't threaten them it's a whole lot easier selling them something. One look at Boyle and you know he couldn't sell heroin to a junkie."

"Uh, Mister Weiss—"

"Later, Boyle. Now, that's my point. Dress down! Let them think you're harmless, and you can sneak up on them. Then... *whammo!* A sale!" Weiss slapped Boyle on the head, meaning to pat him but carried away with enthusiasm at having such a splendid example of innate wimpdom within reach. "You'll be fine, Boyle. It was a figure of speech. Now. About your suit..."

Taken off the griddle, Paulie relaxed. Experience taught him that his turn wasn't due for another hour, at least. He opened his sketchpad and got back to his real work, only now and then glancing at Weiss and nodding to show attention. For two hours he sat and listened to Weiss maunder on about manipulating the client—hints for proper demeanor, dress, attitude, whatever Weiss thought Machiavellian enough to be useful to salesmen filled to the ears with Dale Carnegie and in need of yet more manipulative cant.

Paulie was working the problem of combining two shades of pink with a deep red—difficult, without creating a clash—when silence settled over him and implied trouble. He raised his eyes to find Weiss, and all the trainees but Mike, staring his way. No face offered the slightest hint; Boyle had stopped blushing, so the issue of bow ties had probably been resolved to someone's satisfaction. No other topic defined itself.

"Well?" Weiss demanded. "Are you sleeping, Bradley?"

Paulie slumped in relief, then stretched a leg sideways to kick Mike's ankle.

Mike shook his head. "I don't see a way out," he said aloud. He dropped his hand and sighed. His eyes were red-rimmed and weary. "It's a damn shame."

Weiss squinted at him. He glanced around to see whether any of the others understood what he didn't. (His glance caught and obliterated Boyle's smirk.) "It is, huh? 'Damn shame'?"

"What? Oh, I'm sorry," Mike said. "I guess I drifted away there for a minute." His apology sounded sincere enough. "It's my aunt. Actually, my great aunt. I spent the night sitting up with her and didn't get much sleep."

"A sick relative." Weiss made his sarcasm graphic with a sneer.

"No, she's as well as can be expected, but you see my uncle—great uncle, really—my Uncle Walt died last week, and he left her without a thing. No savings, no insurance, nothing. I spent the night going through her papers, trying to figure some way out for her, but I still don't know enough. If only someone had talked sense to Uncle Walt. I mean, didn't he have an obligation to her? Do you know how thoughtless that is, leaving your wife unprotected?"

Paulie's eyes lost their glazed look and began to twinkle. He bit through the pink pencil he was chewing and turned away to spit out splinters and hide the expression he couldn't erase.

Weiss cocked his head for one more suspicious moment, then relaxed. "It doesn't surprise me. That's the very kind of thoughtlessness that led me to the profession. There are people who need our help."

Mike stared his admiration at Weiss, till he was certain that the man felt self-inspired enough to continue without adulation. Then he propped his shielding hand in front of his eyes. "Tell me when it's my turn again, will you?" he whispered to Paulie. "I've got two orphaned cousins I haven't dragged out yet." He slumped in his chair and fell asleep.

As the morning session ended, Weiss pulled Mike aside for a dollop of heartfelt advice, only a few moments worth but long enough to have Paulie Klein dancing with anticipation as he waited for Mike beside a bank of elevators.

"Come on, give. What was it about?"

Mike shrugged. "He wanted details of my aunt's problem. Maybe he can help, he said, though if you want the truth I think he was feeding his ghoulishness. He also told me he was pleased with the way I've been 'taking ahold.'"

"Ahold of what?"

"I didn't ask."

Snorting, Paulie shook his head. "I know you're not hungover, not on one glass of dago red, but I won't go for the sick aunt routine, either. Don't kid me now, man. How come you look so beat today?"

As they left the Heritage Building, Mike explained, "Just a project I worked out, and it kept me up a while. I'll tell you about it, if you can skip lunch."

"Can't we talk about it while we eat?"

"If you're interested, we've got to go see a man."

"Interested?" Paulie stopped. "Should I be?"

"You're in it."

"No shit?"

"It can't work without you."

"How do I know if I'm interest. . . . Okay, I'm interested. See? You just talked me into it. Something to do with Lester-the-thief, right?"

Mike nodded. He grabbed Paulie's arm and turned him aside, through a knot of people hurrying past, and down the subway steps. "The important part is, it could be worth a nice, easy piece of change. More money than a month of peddling insurance."

"A thousand? I could sure use a thousand for a project. Oh, you know. I told you about my one-man show."

Mike said, "Maybe ten times that, maybe twenty."

"Beautiful! I'm in."

"As easy as that?"

"All right, then. A couple of questions. Is it legal?" He shrugged an apology at Mike's quick look. "Sorry. Skip it. . . . Is it dangerous?"

"Not if we do it right."

"It won't get Lester or any of the big guys, like—say—The Company, pissed at us, will it?"

"Nope. Small bit of private enterprise, harmless to everyone, quiet, no rough stuff, no risks."

Paulie grinned. "I could tell about you the first time I heard you bullshitting Weiss. You sit there like a librarian, playing it cool, but inside you've got everything all mapped out ahead of time. Like, this morning. When Weiss woke you up, that song-and-dance about your aunt—when did you think of that?"

Smiling, Mike said, "Before I went to sleep."

"I knew it! And then.... Oh, I'm out of change. Your treat." Paulie backed away from the subway turnstile and motioned for Mike to feed the coin slot. "Okay, then, for half of X dollars, I'm in. Only... one favor?" At Mike's nod, he said, "No details, okay? Nothing written, nothing to memorize. Just tell me what to do, a step at a time."

Conversation became impossible as the Broad Street subway train arrived squealing behind a cloud of airborne debris and dust. They pushed into the sullen mob inside and stood grinning at each other, shouting unheard non-sequiturs until Mike led the way from the car ten minutes later.

Climbing toward daylight, Mike said, "No details? How can you be sure you'll go along?"

"Listen. I know me. I talk too much. You tell me a secret, first thing I do is find nine people to impress with it. So we're better off if I don't know squat about the whole thing till we pull it off. And then I'm in too deep to say much. Let me have it one step at a time. If you know it'll work, I'm in."

Mike knew his plan was workable; and he'd rather not share the details with anyone else—not Paulie, not Harry, not even Lee—though he needed all three to make it work. Still, in Paulie's instant acceptance, he heard an implied note of reserve.

"You'll go along, you said... until what?"

"Until I get scared," Paulie admitted. "That's another thing I know about me." He searched memory for an example. "You know the ride at Ocean City, the one they call 'The Whip'?"

"Uh-huh."

"Scares hell out of me. That's why I ride it every time I go down the shore. I like being scared. At the same time I'm scared of being scared. Once I even tried joining the paratroops, and that would scare me green. I tried, only they said I'm too short." He grinned and then confessed. "The thing is, when I went to join up, I was counting on them saying that."

Mike laughed. "You've got a deal. If the whole thing starts looking chancy, we'll both get scared and call it off. Well—there it is." He pointed down the block at a large sign, rotating atop an octagonal, marble-faced building. Colonial Cadillac. "I want a few minutes to talk with one of the salesmen. While I'm doing that, you scout around and see what it'll take to break into the place."

Paulie stopped. "Break in? You mean, like forcing a door?"

"How do I know? But I've got the feeling—don't take this wrong, now. I've got the feeling you might know more about breaking in there than I would."

"I might. Do you care how we get inside?"

"Nope." Mike shrugged. "Any way at all. I know why, but—"

"Don't tell me!"

"—but I won't tell you. I know why; it's up to you to figure out how. Find us a door or window without an alarm, some way of getting in and out so nobody knows. We won't take anything. I just want to look the place over, from the inside, without being rushed."

"Scares the hell out of me already." Paulie grinned and stood as tall as possible. "So . . . Geronimo!"

Herb Calder, used car manager of Colonial Cadillac, strolled idly along a row of used cars parked on the Colonial lot. He watched one of the lot-boys in pressed gray coveralls buffing the waxed sheen of a crippled but clean-looking Corvette, until the pair of kids walking toward the lot caught his eye. After four days without a sale, his hundred-a-week guarantee was looking pretty small. If he didn't unload one of these hogs fast he'd be out hunting work. And none of it his fault. How do you sell cars off a lot where they're all overpriced by sixty to seventy percent? Thirty, even forty, no trouble; it gives a man dickering room, but King Kolchak, the dumb-jock owner of Colonial, was cement-block dense, Calder thought. "The higher you run the price the better the car must be," Kolchak said. He didn't have to peddle the damn things. Herb Calder did.

He sauntered, out of the corner of his eye watching the young kids walk closer. One of them wore a suit and looked responsible enough, someone Calder could tie to a five-year financing package without worrying about repossessing the first month. The other one? A weirdo dressed like some cowboy, black spaghetti for hair and a sketchpad under one arm. The kind you have to watch or they'll lift a hubcap when you turn your back. They were kicking tires, peering inside cars on the front row—nineteen three-ton gas gulpers crammed with options. It all depended, Calder thought, on which one was the buyer. They weren't shoppers, he could tell at once. Something serious on their minds. The buckskin one couldn't handle the payments on anything up front. Back row for him,

"Economy Transportation," guaranteed for sixty miles or sixty minutes, whichever came first. The tall one, now, he was a possible.

Calder turned his back to them, freshened his breath with a squirt of Binaca, licked his lips, nodded toward Detroit in prayer, and spun back to face them, 1,000-watt smile in place. "See anything you like?"

"Maybe." Mike Bradley pointed at a Chevrolet Caprice beside them. "What year is this? It looks almost new?"

"It is. Eleven thousand miles. On a car this size, that's barely broken in good."

"But who'd trade in something this new?"

Calder's smile became easier; they were about to get chummy. "Tell you the truth, I wouldn't. But you know how some people are. They can't stand to see a car get dusty before they get the hots to trade it in." Calder showed his manicure. "My name's Herb Calder."

"How are you?" Mike shook hands and turned away.

"What do you think of her?" Calder asked Paulie Klein.

"Out of my class. Let me look around some." He wandered toward the back of the lot, cheering Calder by confirming his earlier guess.

"And anyway"—Calder had to get Mike's attention again—"It was traded in on a new El Dorado. That's reason enough, some might say. When you step up a notch, you've got to give to get."

"Looks pretty nice."

Calder let the car sell itself. He followed Mike around it, answering questions and eliciting information of his own. He found out, or thought he did, that the kid was a stockbroker named Carleton Weiss who lived out in Haverford. Things looked better all the time.

"Could I bring my wife in to drive it?" Mike asked.

"Better than that. Why don't we hop in and drive it out to her? That'd be a real treat, give you a chance to try it on the road."

"She's not home now," Mike said. He thought a moment. "You're sure it's in good shape?"

"Listen." Calder rested a hand on Mike's shoulder and grew confidential. "In this business, there's lots of salespeople think they're sharpies, you know? But they don't last. They really don't. I'm proud to say anyone I place in a car becomes a friend. And you don't make friends by misleading them, know what I mean?"

"That's true," Mike said. "That's a good point."

From behind a four-year-old Dodge on the back row, Paulie watched the laying on of hands. He knew Mike had the salesman hooked. They would never miss him, so he drifted toward the side of the building. Here, nearest the lot, four windows covered with wire mesh looked out from the shop area. Through the grime-stained glass Paulie could see three service men—all in gray coveralls—watching a fourth change a tire. In the backseat of a Sedan de Ville a fifth man slept. No one else in sight. But also no obvious way for him and Mike to get in, unless they felt like breaking through the wire screens.

He ducked around the back of the building, past an open shop double door, down the alley. As he sauntered past he glanced into the service area. It connected with the showrooms through a single door that stood ajar at the moment but was probably locked at night. Nothing here, either.

Then he found a hole in Colonial Cadillac's defenses.

A hollow deal door opened out into the alley from the back of the building. It stood open in the sunshine, revealing a short hallway that led to the glossy, carpeted showroom. The lock looked easy enough—simple night latch and knob-key combination; and near the top of the door, an alarm contact. He was staring at it when footsteps sounded behind him.

He dropped his sketchpad and bent to tie his shoelaces before remembering that he was wearing boots. But the charade seemed to satisfy a young girl who excused herself as she tripped past him balancing a cardboard tray loaded with Big Macs.

He watched her legs till she rounded a counter out of sight, then took advantage of his position to look the alarm over again. When the door closed contact was made between the small alarm box beside the doorframe and a stud in the door itself. A moment's visual search located the painted conduit covering the wire that led down the outside of the building, through a collared hole in the stucco, and into the shop area. The master alarm system would be in there.

Smiling, pleased with himself, Paulie finished not tying his nonexistent bootlaces and rose. He walked whistling from the shade of the shop building into the glare of the lot.

At Calder's desk, Mike continued his con. "This is really nice of you, Herb. It's not that I question your word, you—"

"Of course not, perfectly all right. No sense taking a chance. I'll . . . Here it is." Calder fished through a desk drawer and brought out a gray metal box filled with three-by-five cards. "I keep them all in here," he said. "When Herb Calder says 'one-owner cars,' that's what he means. Let me see, now."

While Calder flipped through the cards, Mike surveyed the showroom. Calder's desk occupied a rear corner, no man's land near but not in an alcove that held a water cooler sweating with condensation. Nearer the street and the broad expanse of gleaming plate glass across the front of the showroom were three more desks where the new-car salesmen, three white-haired men in their sixties, sat erect and stared at passersby. In the middle of the showroom on a rotating platform stood a midnight blue Coupe de Ville. It glistened in the light of small, discreet spotlights perched high above a molding that bordered the room over the windows. Muzak crooned from somewhere. And across the hushed room a counter marked off a work area where two secretaries sat munching lunch while a bald man lacking only an eyeshade to define him worked with a spreadsheet awash with numbers flickering across his PC screen. There was a Xerox machine beside the secretaries' desks, a coffee machine paneled in oak fiberboard near the counter, two black crushed velvet couches, and a reading lamp beside a low table covered with magazines and brochures of one sort or another. All in all, a pleasant place. Except for the revolving car in the middle of the room it might have been a hotel lobby or the foyer of an exclusive club.

"Here it is. Hurley. William Hurley. And here's the phone number." Calder held out the card for Mike to read. "Traded in only four days ago. No, make that five. Why not give him a call? He'll tell you what kind of shape the Caprice is in."

Mike dug his cell phone out of his pocket.

Calder's expression was only slightly pained. "Please," he said, motioning toward the white French phone on his desk. "Use mine. I have to see one of my assistants anyway." He walked away, with great determination not turning back to watch Mike make the call.

Paulie walked in. "Hey," he whispered. "You about done?"

Mike nodded, punching the phone number pad with a pencil while his other hand depressed the cradle. He pantomimed attentiveness, then hung up shaking his head. "Nobody home!" he called out.

Calder trotted back smiling. At the sight of Paulie there, standing on the carpet with his boot heels sinking into the nap, he winced but controlled his urge to tell this freak to shove off. "What did he say?"

"Nobody there," Mike told him. "Listen, I'll try him from my office, and then my wife and I can come back—"

"Now wait," Calder interrupted. If you let them out the door they never come back; and he felt desperation climbing the nape of his neck at the recognition that this one was escaping. "Let me try—"

"Really. I'll stop back later." Mike dropped the printed card on Calder's desk and walked out, Paulie trailing along puzzled.

Calder choked over futile words of persuasion. He turned and kicked the leg of his desk in anger. One of the white-haired men at the front window gave him a curious glance and earned a raised finger for his curiosity.

"Did you get what you wanted?" Paulie asked as they walked toward the subway entrance.

"Enough. And you?"

Without explaining how he knew what to look for, Paulie described how easy it would be to open the back door, bypassing the simple alarm system. Mike nodded, taking mental notes. He stopped to stare at the tenth story of a five-story building across the street. After a moment he said, "Good. Wait a minute," and flipped open his cell phone to place a call, while Paulie stood fidgeting outside.

"What was that all about?"

"Nope. No details. I just had to call Lee and give her a shopping list. We'll need a few things before we go back in there tonight."

"Tonight?" Paulie stared.

"Are you busy?"

"No, but . . . Do we really have to—"

"We really have to."

"Okay." Paulie looked around as if hoping someone would interrupt him before he finished agreeing. When nothing miraculous happened to save him, he said, "You say when, I'll be there."

As part of her continuing effort to get Harry out of the apartment and bolster his sagging spirits, Lee insisted that he accompany her on a set of errands Mike had phoned home to describe. Her insistence created a problem: Harry didn't know that he had sagging spirits, except when he was forced, against his every wish, to get out of the apartment.

"You have any idea what the temperature is out there this time of year?" Harry said. "What it could do to me?"

"It's probably eighty, and it'll do you good to get out."

"A lot you care," Harry muttered. But he went along, bundled in a raccoon coat pulled snug around the girth of two sweaters and a muffler. "Besides, the air isn't fit to breathe, I'll miss my programs—"

"The car has a radio."

"And what happens if I get a coughing spell?"

"I'll try and ignore it. Now, just get in the car."

Before Lee could circle to the driver's side, Harry was belted in and pounding the silent radio with a frustrated fist.

"Wait till I turn the key on," Lee said, smiling at the martyrdom Harry wore like a hair shirt.

They followed Sansom Street west through Center City, crossed the Schuylkill River and continued west toward the shopping area near 69th, every block of the entire route measured by Harry's grousing. He saw no reason for them to leave the apartment. They could just as well have phoned an order to one of the stores nearby and let a delivery boy risk his health in the open air. He couldn't hear the radio with so much traffic noise all around him. Why should he be chasing off Godknowswhere after Godknowswhat? Lee made the mistake of asking what she thought was a rhetorical question.

Harry answered it. "What do you mean, 'take notes'? Even if I could hear what they're saying"—he turned the radio volume lower to make his lament more persuasive—"I couldn't write in this Jap toy car. We've bounced from hell to breakfast for the past mile. I can feel the liver pains starting up again, and it's Mike's fault. If he wasn't so damn cheap he'd buy an American car that didn't jounce your guts out over every little cobblestone."

By way of answer Lee spun the radio volume up full. The rest of the way to 69th Street they rode surrounded by a din impressive enough to shame a foundry. They also collected curious stares each time they stopped at a traffic light, as pedestrians craned to locate the loudspeaker truck they could hear approaching, only to drop down off tiptoe and peer disbelieving into the beige Honda.

When Lee stopped before a long row of specialty shops and switched off the engine, she and Harry both flinched from the sudden blast of silence. "All right, this is it. Here's your list. Take it across to the hardware store, and I'll meet you back here when you're done."

Harry skimmed the list. "All this? Who's going to carry it? You don't expect a man with my back to—"

"Either that, or you can visit The Knitting Boutique over there while I pick up stuff at the hardware store."

"Knitting Boutique? Me? Not on your life!"

"That's what I thought. Try to hurry, will you?"

Harry walked into the hardware store and slammed his fist to the counter. By itself, the paper shopping list wouldn't slam, and he needed the satisfaction of some noise.

With raised eyebrows a young man behind the counter took the list, then made several trips to different areas of the store, fetching and carrying. When he'd finished, the counter between him and Harry held a set of stenciling letters, a pair of wire cutters, two spray cans of black paint and a pint of yellow, two paint brushes, a mop and bucket, ten feet of copper wire, masking tape, and two pairs of rubber gloves. Harry tossed the smaller items into the bucket, paid and got a receipt, hoisted the bucket in one hand, the mop in the other, and left. But not before he had the satisfaction of sneezing toward the clerk.

He was smiling when he got back to the car. Lee wasn't there yet. By hurrying to pile his purchases in the backseat and get settled, eyes closed, he could pretend to have waited a long while for her, though in fact she trotted out of The Knitting Boutique only moments later, carrying a small package.

"Can we go home now?"

"Couple more stops," Lee said.

"As long as I've got to go through this nonsense, you can at least tell me why we're collecting all these things."

"I don't have any idea." Lee was cheerful about her ignorance.

"And you didn't ask?"

"Mike knows what he's doing."

"I don't know why you let him run your life."

"Oh, Daddy, we've been all through this. He's not running my life. It's just... Mike knows what he's doing."

"Hunnnh!" Harry twisted around to pick up the parcel Lee had tossed into the backseat. It contained several small squares of felt and a cellophane envelope stuffed with tiny felt letters. "These, too? Does he know what he's doing with these?"

"He better, 'cause I sure don't."

"Whose money is it we're throwing around like King Midas, answer me that one!"

"Mine. I sold a bedspread."

"Oh." Stumped for another complaint, Harry wheezed several times and settled back to sulk. He sat sullen while Lee entered a costume shop and pretended not to know her when she returned to the car wearing a black, handlebar mustache that didn't quite hide her grin. She carried another one, reddish-brown.

She flipped the mustaches into the backseat with their other purchases and said, "One more stop. This time we both go."

It was Ira's Army-Navy Store, rubber life rafts and boots sprawled across the dust-filled folds of an open parachute in the streaked display window. Harry and Lee walked inside, and into a dark clutter of stacked, wooden bins obscured by a screen of drifting cigar smoke. The smoke issued from a squat man seated behind a counter on a stool, peering at them as if they had come to examine his books. "I'm Ira. Whaddaya want?"

"To start with, put out that cigar."

"Daddy," Lee whispered. "Please."

Ira's jaw fell open, and the cigar fell inside his half-buttoned vest. A brief, frantic dance later, he retrieved his cigar from the floor, and some of his dignity by climbing back onto the stool. "Just who the hell do you think you are?"

"I'm a customer, and that rope you're smoking makes me sick. You ought to be more thoughtful for other—"

"If you're gonna be sick, do it somewhere else. And you!" Ira jumped erect to wave his cigar as a threat. "Get back up that ladder!"

Lee and Harry peered up into the blue haze to see a black gnome at least seventy years old crouched above their heads on a wheeled ladder linked to a track that ran along the bins behind them.

"He's right about the smoke, Ira. Down there, you don't know, but it gets something fierce up here next to the ceiling. I been saying it for fifteen years."

Ira talked to his own upturned palms. "Wouldn't that frost you? Who's running this place, all of a sudden? The customers give orders, the help starts mouthing off. I don't know why I don't just pack it up. I don't need this aggravation. I could get a nice room at the poorhouse, but me . . . me, I got a responsibility. I got my stock to watch. Does anyone ever think about that? 'Take a week off, Ira,' they say. 'Get a rest.' Now it's 'stop smoking cigars'!" He thrust his jaw toward Harry. "You want to buy something, or you come in here to give me an attack? . . . And you, Homer, you get your ass back up that ladder like I said. I want all those hunting boots down here before we close tonight."

"Don't get in a sweat, Ira." The old man climbed again, muttering, "Take 'em down, put 'em back. Wear the things out just handling 'em, if you ask—"

"MOVE!" Ira slammed his palms to the counter top . . . and smiled, as the ladder shimmied under the weight of the stockman scrambling higher.

"Please?" Lee pushed in ahead of Harry. "We'd like some gray coveralls. Two pair."

Willing to forgive and forget, Ira slumped back to his stool and avoided Harry's glare. "Gray coveralls. What size?"

"One for me, and one for him," Lee said, tapping her father on the shoulder.

"Me? Why should I have to wear those things?"

"Quiet, Daddy. You're Mike's size, is all." Then, to Ira, "Is that all right?"

Ira shrugged. "It's okay by me. You pay, I'll sell you whatever I got, if I got it. But that don't answer the question. Size, I said. Now, this teddy bear here is so wrapped up in fur, I couldn't guess his size on a bet."

"What do you mean, 'teddy bear'? Lee, ask him what he—"

"Tell your boyfriend to cool down, Miss, and we can get some business done here. Believe it or not, I'm not running a day-care center for cuckoos."

"He's not my boyfriend, he's my—"

"You're smart not to admit it."

"—my father. He wears a size forty-two long."

Ira snorted. "Hey, Frank! We got some gray coveralls in a forty-two long?"

The wrinkled, black face stared down in bewilderment. "What's that mean, 'forty-two long'? We got medium and small, and maybe a large in white, if he drives an ice cream truck or something."

Nodding, Ira talked around his cigar butt and showed them his palms again. "There you are. Medium, or small. Now you decide which is forty-two long, medium or small."

Lee was doubtful. "Medium, I think. Daddy, would you try it on?"

"Undress? Here?"

"That's a point, Miss. Your old man's right. Y'see it's after three now, and we close at five thirty. Now I figure, for him to peel off his furs and put on some coveralls, that would take him till nine or ten tonight, at least."

"How would you like it if I took that cigar away from you?"

"Now please, both of you.... Daddy, come here a minute." Lee led Harry away, whispering to him. She left him standing by the open front door, inhaling with great vigor and displaying his most practiced show of lofty irritation. A Doberman sniffing a circle around the fire hydrant outside paused to look him over, then bolted when Harry hissed at him.

"Medium will be fine," Lee said. "Do you think a small will fit me?"

Ira surveyed her from shoulder to knee. "Well, I'd say so. But—excuse me now for saying this, but you're... uh... you're kind of filled out, you know? Maybe a medium wouldn't be so tight across the...." His hand pawed at his own chest in demonstration.

"Daddy!" Lee warned her father, who restrained his urge to charge and contented himself with coughing out the doorway, startling the Doberman now standing on three legs beside a lamppost. The dog hopped away, hind leg still lifted. And inside the store the crisis had passed.

"Why don't I try it on? Is there a...?" She peered into the gloom of the store.

"Here?" Ira grinned. "There's no dressing room, if that's what you're asking. My customers, they're not what you'd call style-conscious. But you can go behind the row of shelves, on the other side. No windows over there."

Now Harry did attack. Pointing up, he shouted, "You keep on this side of the shelves, you up there!"

Ira was indignant. "What are you, Mister, some kind of bigot? You think because my partner's black he's going to cop a peek at your kid? Homer, he's been past all that sex stuff for twenty years. Right, Homer?"

"Past it, right," Homer nodded. "You get to my age, whatever don't hurt, don't work.... Only thing is, if you want to know the truth, I do like to look once in a while."

"Maybe I'll chance the size," Lee said. "One medium, and one small." She waited while Ira wrapped them in brown paper and made change. "Come on, Daddy." She picked up the package and left.

Harry started after her but was seized by a coughing spell. Apologetic, coughing so much that he was unintelligible, he walked back to the counter and asked for a drink of water.

"To get rid of you, anything." Ira drew a paper cup of tan water from a dingy cooler behind him and handed it over.

With one delicate, firm hand, Harry snatched the cigar from Ira's mouth, dunked it in the water, and ran.

Lee watched him sprint from the shop door, stumble over the Doberman poised on three legs beside a bark-poor plane tree, and scramble to the car. As she drove away, Harry's coughless laughter filled the Honda. In her rearview mirror she could see Ira in his doorway, waving and shouting something, while the cowed Doberman—whimpering now—hobbled away on stiff legs. He was crying.

Mike Bradley pressed Paulie's cell phone against his cheek and listened to its distant ring. He had rehearsed this call a dozen times. All that work might be useless, because only his half of the conversation was predictable; and now he shuffled through his main arguments. When a voice said, "Hello?" he asked for Lester. "Tell him it's Mike with the beige Honda." While he waited, he stared out the window.

He was calling from Paulie Klein's two-room loft over the empty warehouse, and he could see across the street, between a pair of piers, the night traffic on the Delaware River. Red and green running lights of small boats. The searchlight of a Coast Guard cutter cruising past the loading docks and making visual spot checks. Miles beyond the scene in front of him, across the Delaware in New Jersey, Lester was being summoned to the phone. While Mike waited, people were moving toward him. Without knowing it, they were also moving toward the coming weekend and the plan he had worked out. If this call went well.... He refused to consider the alternative. One step at a time.

Focusing on the reflections in the glass windowpane, he could see Paulie and Lee behind him, seated on the floor, watching. The sound of their breathing defined the tension they felt. Mike didn't turn around to face them. He shrugged stiffness out of his back and stood relaxed, hips canted, to let them see confidence. "They're getting Lester now," he said.

Lee squirmed sideways over the worn carpet nearer Paulie. They sat Indian-fashion on the floor and until moments before had been sewing small letters onto a felt background. Watching Mike, they let their hands slow, and then stop. Now, they waited.

"Lester? This is Mike Bradley.... Sure you do. I came with Paulie Klein the other.... That's right, the Honda. Remember what we were talking about? Well, I've got a proposition for you.... I know, but listen a minute. Suppose someone wanted to sell a new Cadillac, let's say to raise money in a hurry for an operation, or... well, any reason. Sell it quick. What do you think he might get for it?... That's right.... I understand that, but I was hoping you might know of someone in the market for such a car.... No, no. New. Say, no more than a couple thousand miles on it and a clean title.... Uh-huh.... Uh-huh, that sounds interesting. Let's say I phone Saturday and discuss it again.... You'd be making a mistake, Lester. I don't joke about things like this.... Fine, then. Saturday."

Mike folded the phone and stared out the window, his face hidden from the watching pair behind him.

Paulie bounced on the floor with excitement. "Give, man! What did he say?"

Mike turned to face them, and to offer the grin he wore. "We got him going. He's figured me for some kind of nut kid trying to pretend he's got a line on a hot deal, but he's not sure. When I teased him a little you could hear him drooling into the phone. We talked about a hypothetical friend of his who might want to buy a new Caddy... cheap. He—"

"You can see that," Paulie protested. "You know how careful Lester is. What if his phone's bugged, or mine is? He's got to stay cool and—"

"Let him tell it!" Lee nodded. "Go ahead, Mike. What did he say?"

"About what I figured. A brand-new car, with the title, he'll go three thousand. But now he's laughing at the whole idea with Camille and Lucille. Or, part of him is. Part of him hopes we pull it off. Let's see how he laughs this Saturday."

"Great!" Paulie hugged himself, and then on second thought hugged Lee. He asked her, "You ever walk down a dark stairway with a door closed at the bottom? Even in the dark you can 'feel' the door ahead of you—I don't know how—and you try to feel just when you're going to bump into it, right?"

"I guess so."

"That's what's happening now. I haven't got the faintest damn glimmer of where we're going. I can feel the door getting closer, and it scares the hell out of me!"

"I get it. Any second now, POW! Right into the door."

"That's it. POW!" Paulie whirled and threw his needlework at the wall. It fluttered to the floor six feet short.

"Hey, don't lose the disguise." Mike retrieved the piece of felt and handed it back. "Over the left pocket," he told Lee, while she shook the folds out of the smaller pair of gray coveralls. "It's almost ten. By the time you finish that, we can shove off."

"Let me get my sketchpad." Paulie scrambled to his feet.

"You won't need it, believe me."

Eyes big and serious, Paulie said, "Maybe not. But where I go, it goes. You ever hear of industrial espionage? More than one guy would love to get his hands on my designs, and I don't let that pad out of my sight."

Mike and Lee watched Paulie walk into his bedroom before Lee said, "He's a little weird, isn't he?"

"Only a little."

"'Swhat I said."

"So's everybody else. Just in different ways."

They parked in an alley mouth half a block from the Colonial Cadillac showrooms. The glow of streetlamps and neon washed out the stars overhead. Distant sirens sounded from nearer the river. While Paulie unloaded gear from the trunk of the Honda and stowed his sketchpad where Lee could guard it for him, Mike explained and Lee understood her role.

"I've got it, I've got it," she said. "Twenty minutes from now I'll be right here, waiting."

"If a squad car starts down the alley..."

"I pull around in front, blinking the lights."

"Perfect." He motioned for Paulie to follow along and ducked into the dark alley.

"Wait up," Paulie said, panting behind him. "You've got legs like a giraffe, and I'm lugging all this stuff. How about carrying the mop?"

"Wearing Harry's good suit? Sorry, Paulie, but that's the way the world goes. Workers work, and executives... exec."

"I knew there was a reason I had to wear this get-up." Paulie shrugged to loosen the stiff gray coverall binding his arms. Over the breast pocket a small red oval bore smaller green letters in a pair of arcs, on top and on bottom, reading "Colonial Cadillac." It was the uniform he had seen that afternoon on all the mechanics. "The big pair of coveralls fit you. Why couldn't I wear a suit and have the cushy job?"

"It's another sad fact. Executives are taller than workers, don't ask me why. I don't make the rules, Paulie. I'm taller, so I wear the suit and tie."

"Maybe, but it's dark here, and no one would see you ruin the image. At least carry the mop."

"Too late. There's the door."

Paulie dropped his load of gear and fished two pairs of rubber gloves out of the bucket. After he and Mike donned them, he used a flashlight to point out the conduit that traced the doorframe, and they got to work. The silhouette of the Honda defined the nearer alley entrance. At the opposite end, the headlights of passing cars swept by as flickering punctuation that kept distracting them. Traffic noises surrounded the block—distant squealing brakes and a punctured muffler's throaty growl—creating the eerie feeling that only where they were, only inside a six-foot circle, was there silence; and even that silence was broken by the scrape of pliers along stucco and tin.

It took scant seconds to peel back two sections of the flimsy tin conduit, one on each side of the door near the ground. While Mike watched the alley mouth and the back of buildings to their left, Paulie scraped insulation off the alarm wire. He twisted an end of coiled copper wire into the exposed alarm system at each bare spot. In a moment the connections were made.

"Here goes," Paulie whispered. Just above the connection beside the door on their right he snipped the alarm wire. And they waited in a tense crouch.

Nothing happened.

A dog barked somewhere nearby, but nothing else. The circuit remained intact, shunted to bypass and eliminate the door alarm from the system.

Paulie giggled, then cleared his throat. He couldn't keep the sound of a smile out of his boasting. "I told you it would work. Nothing to it."

"Sure, unless you break the wire standing on it."

"What?" Paulie lunged backward then shook his head at Mike's chuckle. "Hey, that's not funny! If we break that shunt all hell's going to tear loose, either in the garage where the main board is—I think—or at the precinct house."

"I'll watch it, Paulie. Just show me how we beat the lock on the doorknob." Mike held the coiled wire loose in one hand out of the way.

Paulie slipped a credit card between the door and the frame, leaned his weight against the door and slid the card up against the night latch. And pushed. And lifted. And nothing happened. After a moment's pause . . . nothing happened, again. Paulie said, "There's another way." Like a ballet dancer at the exercise bar, he rested a hand on Mike's arm and raised one booted foot. The foot lashed out and slammed against the doorknob. It took three kicks till the wood surrounding the knob splintered and the hollow door gave way. With a sound like newspaper crumpling, the knob and lock mechanism popped out of sight, through a new hole that cast a shaft of yellow light into the alley.

And the door swung open.

"After you, Executive." Paulie bowed Mike inside.

Mike pushed the door shut behind them and plugged the revealing hole with his crumpled handkerchief. A short hallway led toward the showroom. Visible at the end of the hall was a reception area, the corner of one velvet couch and a table, with the showroom window beyond it. Left of the couch a counter separated the secretaries' area from the carpeted showroom, and halfway down the hallway, a door marked the entrance to the garage. Paulie ducked into the garage and was back in a moment, whispering, "All the alarms are shut off at the panel."

"Now what?"

"I've got to copy some names and addresses, fifteen minutes, tops. While I'm doing that, you mop the floors."

"Why not just duck in, grab what you want, and go?'

Mike motioned Paulie forward toward the showroom. "I want some information without tipping what it was we came in after. Besides, take a look."

The showroom ahead of them blazed with light. The Coupe de Ville on its platform had stopped rotating, the Muzak was stilled, but otherwise the agency looked open for business. "They leave the showroom lights on at night. It's better if we amble through the job and let anyone passing by think we belong here—just a couple of people working late. An eager young executive, and..."

"Uh-huh. The janitor. Okay, but maybe this once you goofed. Do you really expect me to get out there in the spotlights with this mop and pretend I'm mopping the carpet?"

"People see what they think they see. The carpet doesn't show from the street. Would you rather have toted a vacuum cleaner up the alley?"

"Okay, all right, I'll mop. You do whatever the hell you're here for; only don't be all night about it. I've had my share of 'scared' for the next month."

They paused a moment longer but neither could think of anything more to delay what had to be done, then Mike walked into the bright lights, past the Coupe de Ville, to Herb Calder's desk.

Paulie trailed along, with heavy exaggerated gestures setting the mop in motion.

Calder's desk wasn't locked, a piece of luck that cheered Mike at once. He found the small card file and a tablet in the desk. Calder had pointed out all the names, people who'd traded their cars in on new Cadillacs and could vouch for the condition of their trade-ins. Mike sat behind the desk and began to copy names and addresses, and dates of purchase.

Paulie tried whistling while he dragged the dry mop back and forth over the thick-napped carpet. His lips stuck to his teeth and his best pucker seemed clogged with dust. He managed nothing noisier than a rush of air. He switched to humming. That didn't help either. Across the room Mike sat writing something, while cars went by with terrifying regularity. Paulie felt that each car slowed as it passed, its occupants staring at him and wondering about the idiot misusing the mop. He tried to reason himself out of the mood: only nerves, natural apprehension, Mike had it all figured. What could go wrong? The more he thought about that question, the more answers occurred to him. Everything could go wrong!

When he noticed himself mopping the top of his boots he gave in. "Mike? I don't mean to panic, man, but can you hurry up?"

"Hang in there. I've got to copy these cards."

"Use the damn Xerox machine! I feel like a target out here in these lights."

Even if the copier wasn't much faster, it sat concealed from the street by the counter and desks of the office area. Mike plugged in the machine, raised the rubber cover, and spread a score of note cards on the glass plate with shaking hands. After a moment he spoke over his shoulder. "Either this thing is broken, or it's got to warm . . ."

Paulie looked up at hearing the catch in Mike's voice.

"Better get that mop over here on the bare floor," Mike whispered through the stiff lips of a fake smile. "In front of the counter by the coffee machine. Don't turn around, but we've got company."

Paulie froze, half bent over the mop handle, till curiosity and fear turned his head toward the street. A squad car was parked in front. A patrolman stood outside the main door, watching them. Fear clouded Paulie's vision and he couldn't see the cop's face—didn't want to. He moved to his right and began swabbing the tile floor beside and behind a large coin-operated coffee maker, all the while resisting the urge to sprint for the back door and safety. He felt rather than saw Mike stride to the front door, heard a latch snap.

"Can I do something for you, officer?"

"Working kind of late, aren't you?"

"Second time in the past three weeks. You know how it goes. The work piles up, and the boss sure isn't going to stay late to get it done. Herb Calder's my name. My card?"

Paulie sneaked a glance at them. Mike stood confident in the doorway. The patrolman was reading a business card in his hand.

"Well. Mind telling me what you're doing?"

"Can we step outside a second?"

After a terrifying silence, Paulie risked another glance at the pair outside. Mike and the cop were staring at him, and talking. He bent low, redoubled his efforts at scrubbing with the dry mop. If they wanted to see a janitor at work he could give them that. But in case, just in case, he started mopping his way toward the back door, head bent low.

The click of the door startled him and he heard his own involuntary grunt echo in the still showroom. He straightened up to watch Mike waving at the squad car, which eased away from the curb and into traffic.

Paulie slumped to the velvet couch and dried his palms on the cushions. "Jesus H. Christ! What was that all about?"

Mike held out one trembling hand on display and smiled. "A squeaker," he said. Then, not trusting himself to say anything more, he crossed to the Xerox machine and pushed a button. A bright light flared, the machine whirred and spat out a copy. "Don't ask me the whole thing," he said. "I'm still a little shook. I told the cop we'd been missing money from the coffee machine since you started to work here, and I was staying late to keep an eye on you."

"Me?" Surprise drew Paulie to his feet. "Why me? Why not just tell him—"

"He's a cop, Paulie. His thing is looking for criminals, so I gave him one, and you're it. Then I tried selling him the Corvette out front, and he—"

"You tried selling . . . ? Jesus!"

"That's my thing, remember? I'm a car salesman. He swallowed it, for now. But he'll be back in half an hour. He promised to keep an eye on you, if I leave you here alone when I go. Let's move it." The Xerox machine's light flared again. "I'm about done."

"But he saw us! Tomorrow they'll know someone was in here."

"Right, so take a bunch of the brochures off that table and scatter them around. Make it look like vandalism. Dump out the desk drawers, tip a couple chairs over—but not out front near the window. Make a mess, and hurry."

Paulie protested, "The lights are—"

"Don't panic on me now, Paulie. It's working fine. You're the janitor, keep janiting."

Several deep breaths calmed Paulie. The counter and secretaries' desks hid Mike from view, so long as he stayed bent over the Xerox copier. A few minutes more and they'd be done. He brushed magazines from the table with his mop handle, flipped a pair of cushions from the couch to the floor, and worked his way back to Calder's desk, dragged it into the alcove and scattered the contents of the drawers. The physical work helped, and he could feel his fear melting away, tension turning to enjoyment. He threw papers and magazines, getting his back into his work: paper plates from the coffee counter became sailing frisbees, newspapers fluttered through the air like pigeons. He was whistling and scattering papers when Mike joined him.

"All set?" Mike tossed the box of file cards into the mess on the floor. "They'd have known we were here by the broken back door, anyway, and we can't patch the alarm system together again. If we don't steal anything they'll think it was a prank. Ready?"

Giddy with relief, Paulie tossed the mop aside and started for the back door.

"NO! Take the mop along. We can't leave—"

"You bring it," Paulie said. "I've got an idea, a thing I read abut." He ducked behind the counter into the office area. As if in slow motion, a moment later, his face rose over the counter top, an impish Kilroy. "Ready to haul ass, Executive? Let's give them something to blow their mind."

"What are you—"

"Watch." Paulie stood up, nude. He leapt atop the Xerox machine to lay with his groin over the glass copy window, punched the button; and the instant the light flared around his hips he reached back to unplug the machine in mid-operation.

Before Mike could react to the shock of what he'd seen, Paulie jerked his coveralls back up over his shoulders, zipping them as he snatched up the bucket and sprinted for the back door.

Mike caught him in the alley. "What the hell was that?"

Paulie was laughing too hard to answer. He gasped, "Oh, wait. Wait till they... Well, it's a thing I read about. Use your imagination, man. When they plug in that machine tomorrow, they'll meet the Electronic Flasher—Buck Rogers in a raincoat. They'll never figure we were... that we went in to..." With one last chuckle, Paulie calmed himself. He thought a moment. "Mike, why did we go in there?"

"Let's get to the car and I'll tell you all about it."

"Just the part that comes next. I feel that door down there ahead of us in the dark, and I don't want to know when the smash is coming."

They trotted along the dark alley, Paulie stripping off his rubber gloves and Mike holding the mop in one hand, Xerox copies in the other. A janitor and a young executive, headed home after a hard day's work.

As they opened the car door Lee said, "Mike! A cop went by a few minutes ago, in front. I didn't know what to do."

"I know, Babe. Let's move it. We go to stage two."

WEDNESDAY

On his IRS forms King Kolchak listed his occupation as "Owner, Colonial Cadillac," not so much a lie as a misunderstanding. Two of his three ex-wives knew better but didn't care; their alimony checks kept coming. And wife number four didn't know. She spent her days in the Kolchak mansion in Lower Merion supervising the household help as they polished her husband's trophies. It was a task she knew well. A former trophy-polisher herself, she and King had met in his trophy room one afternoon, and met again later three nights a week to couple on the leopard-skin couch while films of King rampaging through defensive backfields filled the room with their flickering light. They had met there, till wife number three caught them at it. Ex-wife number three now lived in a new Miami condo, and number four supervised her former coworkers in the Kolchak mansion.

For King to misunderstand his position might have been curious a few years, and several hundred off-tackle slants, earlier. But he had come out of the National Football League with a big reputation as a ladies' man, a tarnished reputation as a once-great running back, and scrambled brains. He could feed himself and tie his shoes (but not a necktie) and had enough recall to house a stock of dirty jokes that had somehow survived the battering his skull had undergone. People told him to look for a job in public relations.

Through undeserved great good luck he became instead "Owner, Colonial Cadillac." It beat selling his name to decorate a chain of hot dog stands, like what's-theirnames from the former Colts. There was only one drawback to his job, so far as he could tell. He had to go to his car store four or five days a week.

Accountants came from somewhere and did the books for him to sign, that was okay. Salesmen handled the actual operation of the agency. Two men in wide floral ties brought him messages from the fan who had lent King the money he needed to become "Owner, Colonial Cadillac." In spite of that, Kolchak had to go to work several days a week. A waste of time. He did no work—understanding nothing of what transpired at his 'car store'—watched television, and he could have done that at home as well as in his office. But he forgot these brief touches of pique as easily as he forgot everything else except his total yardage record and jersey number; that is, he forgot his irritation within minutes after finding it lying fresh and surprising within the white uncluttered expanse of his imagination.

King Kolchak was a calm, peaceful man who might have settled for a simpler life than the one he led. His needs were few: food, of course, and sleep; someone to boink three or four nights a week while he watched videotapes or films of himself scampering over the yard-striped grass or Astroturf; and, even more important, order. He disliked being surprised, because surprises confused him.

On the morning when he parked behind Colonial Cadillac and walked to the back door he was surprised, and then confused, at all the commotion he caused by jerking loose a piece of wire that lay on the ground between him and the broken back door of the building. He saw the splintered wood surrounding a hole where the doorknob ought to be, the place where he inserted a key on those mornings when he came to work. Then a piece of wire tangled around his shoe. He snatched up the wire in irritation. Bells began to ring inside the building, and no more than four minutes later, while he was trying to find a switch to stop all the ringing, two keening squad cars squealed to a stop outside. Cops.

"Cops" was a key word for King Kolchak. The fan who had bought him the agency had said over and over (it seemed to Kolchak dozens of times, though in fact it had been hundreds) that he must never, under any circumstances whatsoever, call the cops to his car store. When four uniformed policemen poured into the showroom with guns drawn, a flag went up in Kolchak's mind. Get rid of them. No cops.

He assured them there was nothing wrong, turned on the Kolchak charm, told both his two best jokes—by accident swapping punch lines between them—and gave the cops passes to an Eagles' game. After they left he went out to the alley and picked up the discarded passes to give them away again. He didn't understand why Philadelphians tended to throw Eagles tickets on the ground, and only strangers to the city would keep and use them. He went back inside to phone The Trouble Number, printed on a white card that lay in his otherwise empty top-center desk drawer. He had never called it before—oh, yes, there was that time when the windstorm or something broke the front window. He had only once called it before. He listened to the distant ringing and waited for the fan who had lent him the money, or for one of his assistants, to answer.

Someone did. Kolchak explained about the wire and the broken door and the ringing bells and the policemen and the football passes and found himself talking to a dead phone.

His secretary, Shirley Frazee, and Mary Sloane the receptionist came in. The three old men whose names he could never remember and who sold the new cars came in. He could hear people in the shop next door pounding and making noises. Every so often one person or another poked his head into King's office and asked about the broken back door. Kolchak winked, and nodded, and said everything was fine. They went away.

In less than an hour the men in wide floral ties arrived, along with King Kolchak's principal fan, the man who had bought the agency out of respect for Kolchak's greatness as a running back, Theodore Winthrop.

On paper, on those same IRS forms signed by King Kolchak, "Owner," Colonial Cadillac was thriving. In fact it lost money but thus became all the better a geyser through which The Company's money could spout to the surface. And Theodore Winthrop had great respect and affection for this agency. He loved to watch over it as it floundered and he prospered. His affection was so sincere that it overrode his immense distaste for King Kolchak—a distaste caused in part by the difference in their suit sizes. King Kolchak was an honest six-foot-four, two hundred thirty pounds, and little of it flab.

Winthrop, for all his leonine appearance in photographs, his great thatch of razor-cut and coifed white hair, stood a scant five-foot-eight. He sat as much as possible.

The moment he entered Kolchak's office behind the Guappo brothers in their wide ties, Winthrop sat. "What's it about, King? Why cops?"

"Hard to tell, Mister Winthrop. There was all this ringing. Alarm bells they said, and they came to find out why."

"Have you checked to see what was stolen? Any records, or files? Did they get into your safe?"

Kolchak laughed. "Who'd steal anything from me? You know how my fans—"

"Take a look." Winthrop motioned over his shoulder, and one of his men, Frank Guappo, walked out to talk with the office personnel, all those now feigning work but interested in the meeting behind the frosted glass of Kolchak's office door. Frank's brother Tiger, Winthrop's nominal bodyguard, stood watching his boss and Kolchak.

Like King Kolchak, Tiger Guappo understood little of what was said in the next few minutes. Winthrop talked. Kolchak and Tiger listened. Their silence bothered Winthrop not in the slightest. He did his best thinking, talking aloud, and he was accustomed to being heard. His talking bothered them even less. The three- and four-syllable words he sometimes used created a drone of noise that would have confused either, had either listened. An ex-fighter, Tiger bore few marks from his sixty-four professional bouts, all fixed (nine wins, fifty-five losses, under several aliases). Better than that, he had come through all those fights with less damage to his native intelligence than Kolchak had suffered in the more civilized head-busting of the NFL. But then, Tiger had started his career with an IQ astounding in its minuteness. Though he was for most occupations unemployable, he had two virtues: a willingness to listen to Theodore Winthrop, and a protective older brother who was vicious.

Frank Guappo returned to report nothing stolen. "Looks like kids on a tear. They flung some papers around, is all. I don't think it was nothing important."

"That may be," Winthrop said. "I am still not happy to have one of my places busted open. Kids, punks, no matter. They better know they can't interrupt my affairs. Did you talk to the two girls I saw out front?"

"Nothing about boffing them, just only so far as concerns business, Mister Winthrop."

"That's my meaning, Frank. Let's go talk to them again." He rose and started out, creating a minor panic in the Guappo brothers, who rushed to open the door for him and get out of his way at the same time.

Kolchak had no such problems. He stood flexing his hands, sucked in his stomach, and walked out behind them. After all, it was his car store. If his number one fan wanted to look around the office, that was fine with King.

Neither Mary nor Shirley knew a thing about the break-in. They answered Winthrop's questions in nervous monosyllables, all the while looking to Kolchak for instructions and talking so long as he kept winking permission to them. Winthrop finally dismissed the girls and led Kolchak aside, to the coffee machine, to talk in private.

"I don't like trouble, King. I think you know that."

"There's no trouble here. We're making money, and look." King pointed to a pair of civic awards—"Friends'

Camp Contributor" and "Community Chest Over-the-Top Club"—hanging on the wall beside the coffee machine. "People in town know what the name King Kolchak stands for. If I thought—"

"Fine. Keep it that way." Winthrop didn't look at the award plaques; his money had bought them, and he knew to the dollar what they were worth. "Your fans put up the money for this operation. I know you're not the kind of man to disappoint his fans. Am I right?"

"You can count on me, Mister Winthrop. When they call my number, I—"

"Oh, shit, King! Knock off the numbers stuff. I guess if this is the most serious problem you ever call me about. . . ." Winthrop turned to scan his showroom once more before leaving, then called out, "Frank? Bring Tiger."

Frank sat perched on the receptionist's desk, unable to get her interested in being boffed anytime soon and beginning to turn his attention to the other one, Shirley Frazee, who was displaying her exceptional legs by bending over the Xerox machine to plug it in. "Yes sir," he said, and jumped to his feet. "Tiger?'

Tiger stood where he'd been left, midway between the two office desks, since no one had yet told him either to sit down or to get out of the middle of the small office area. At the sound of his name his eyes focused and his head swung from side to side till he recognized a face. "I'm right here, Frank."

"I know where you are, Tiger. Come on, we're going."

Tiger had one foot lifted when Shirley Frazee's scream startled him into immobility. Frank jumped to catch her as she turned from the Xerox machine, glassy-eyed, and crumpled. He eased her to the floor, cursing. Mary leaped to her feet at the scream and now knelt beside the girl's still body. Pietro Aiello—who rarely lost his composure without also losing his assumed identity—ducked behind the coffee machine and reached for the gun he hadn't carried in the twelve years since he'd become Theodore Winthrop. It was King Kolchak who took command.

Through a misunderstanding.

So little time elapsed between Shirley's little scream and the sight of her in Frank Guappo's arms that Kolchak felt called upon to save the girl's honor, or whatever was threatened by this man in the wide tie. King had pinned a few secretaries to the floor in his own time and wanted none of that going on in his store. In a burst of energy he rested a hand on the counter top and vaulted into the office area, bumping into Tiger Guappo, who was unable to hold his balance, frozen, flamingo-posed on one foot.

King collided with Tiger, who fell over Frank, who sprawled atop Shirley, who wouldn't have minded all that much if he'd bought her a drink or taken her to a movie first.

The lustful picture outraged Kolchak. He shouted an unintelligible grunt, hurled Frank off Shirley and prepared to do battle. He came close to making a serious mistake. There was no friendliness in Frank's smile, less than none in the knife Frank brandished with a deft, flicking wrist.

But Winthrop reappeared from behind the coffee machine. "What the hell is this? Back off. Back off, I said!"

They did, with varying degrees of reluctance, and Winthrop circled the end of the counter to pick up the warm sheet of Xerox copy paper lying beside Shirley's outstretched hand. It showed an 8 1/2 x 11 close-up of Paulie Klein's groin, unremarkable to an accomplished student of male anatomy like Shirley Frazee, but something of a shock to find in your hand at 10:14 of a sunny fall morning.

Kolchak peered over Winthrop's shoulder—easy enough with the difference in their height—and in that moment exceeded his usual daily ration of ideas. "A clue!" he shouted.

Winthrop's glare might have melted glass. It never reached King Kolchak's eyes but passed under his chin to singe Herb Calder, walking into work over an hour late. Calder blanched, recalled his past few days, wheeled, and escaped through the still-closing door. He quit. He could always go back to selling encyclopedias. Or time-shares. Or shoes.

Mike Bradley and Theodore Winthrop had more in common than either of them might have recognized. Both had a gift for detail. Winthrop had converted a mob of semiliterate hoodlums into a corporation whose cash flow rivaled that of most emerging African nations. His corporation, The Company, operated with three sets of books: one on a spreadsheet for the IRS, a single set, no matter that the numbers it displayed were scattered among his sixteen legitimate business firms; a second set displayed in ledgers for the eyes of other shareholders in The Company, Winthrop's lieutenants; and yet a third that existed only in Winthrop's head. He enjoyed manipulating figures—to his own advantage, of course—and looking for flaws in the structure of the high-rise house of cards he had built. It was a game to him. A professional game.

An amateur, Mike Bradley enjoyed a similar game, though he had never named the mental exercises that filled his idle moments. He saw implications that escape most people. Two days after the most recent attack on Israel, his imagination seized upon "Arab oil." He looked for a soft European economy dependent on that oil and in his imagination sold short several Dutch stocks listed on The Hague bourse. A precipitous drop in the Dutch balance-of-trade proved him right, and in less than three weeks he doubled his (imaginary) investment. He toyed with the idea of proposing to Alka-Seltzer the franchising of coin-operated, individual tablet dispensers, to be mounted on telephone poles on any city block that held both a McDonald's and a Pizza Hut. Instead, he invested his Dutch profits in four used Navy helicopters, some bribes, a federal hunting permit, caught wild-horse herds on federal land, and opened a chain of Wranglerburger stands, the week the USDA approved horse meat for human consumption . . . not in fact, but all within the fertile field of his imagination.

No matter how much he enjoyed these exaggerated and complex plots, they remained for him pure entertainment.

Or had remained. Until his conversation with Lester-the-thief. For a few hours after that meeting, he pondered. He knew that everyone has dreams, but that only those few dreamers with real courage pursued their dreams, after dreaming them. The difference wasn't imagination but energy and ambition. Lester's operation, what Mike understood of it, challenged him. Admiring it wasn't enough. He would improve it. Or top it.

Mike Bradley accepted his own challenge.

It brightened a life he hadn't known was drab. Even the training sessions at Heritage Old-Line Fidelity

Insurance took on new meaning as pedestrian contrast to the swirl of true risk—not mere actuarial risk—that sucked him and Lee and Paulie deeper into the vortex of Saturday looming ahead.

Wednesday morning, for example: he and Paulie sat at the conference table in the Heritage Building and planned estates. Given a family of X-size, with Y-retirement aims and Z-educational goals for the (2.5) children, what sort of financial base—in A-savings, B-investments, C-insurance—would balance the equation? Paulie sweated over his set of figures. Mike hummed. Esther Flett had finished her calculations and now sat staring at a new, blank page. If Weiss wanted to think she couldn't keep up, let him think it. Robert Boyle copied answers from the trainee next to him, the man from Ohio State. They'd been handed different problems, with different assumptions and different figures on the page, but Boyle didn't consider that possibility. And Carleton Weiss circled the table peering over shoulders to comment.

"That's it, Bradley," he said. "That's nice and clean."

"It is, isn't it?" Mike couldn't help smiling, though he knew Paulie wouldn't understand his pleasure. But then Paulie didn't know, didn't want to know, the small steps underway out on the street.

Mike assumed that the staff of Colonial Cadillac had by now investigated the break-in and dismissed it as a prank. He imagined faces filled with bewilderment in the brochure-littered showroom, a burst of consternation turning to resigned disgust at the senseless but finally harmless vandalism. By now, 11:00 AM, that was all past, the broken door had been repaired, and business had resumed at Colonial Cadillac. That was one scenario occupying his mind as he played with the interesting numbers before him.

Another scenario involved Lee and Harry Schaeffer. Harry's drone of irritation at the shopping duties he'd performed had blossomed into full martyrdom when he learned that Mike had yet more for him to do. He was to serve as Lee's navigator on a tour Mike had planned.

Mike laughed to recall Harry's reaction.

And Paulie grunted, "What's so funny? If you can do any better, let's see it." He slid his work sheets in front of Mike and leaned close to be instructed.

"One step at a time, Paulie. It works like this."

"He never does anything the easy way, does he?" Harry Schaeffer struggled to refold an open map of Philadelphia spread across his raccoon-swaddled lap. He and Lee sat parked at the corner of Walnut Lane and Greene Street in Germantown, planning their route.

"It's not Mike's fault you can't refold the map. Nobody can. They're all designed to be irrefoldable."

"What?"

"Folding the map."

"No, the route! Look at this." His finger traced a red line drawn on the map, a line that zigzagged through the neighborhoods of Germantown and Chestnut Hill, back down Walnut Lane to Manayunk and Roxborough, then swung out City Line Avenue to the eastern tip of the Main Line suburbs. "He's got us jumping back and forth all over the place."

"He said it's the quickest way to cover them all."

"And you believe him." Harry's tone showed clearly enough what he thought of such misplaced faith.

"He was right about avoiding the one-way street you wanted to use for a shortcut. Now, you just follow the map, and tell me where to turn."

Grumbling, Harry did what Lee asked.

They wandered back and forth over residential streets, past whole blocks of brick twins or rowhouses, out into the cluster of gray stone Victorian mansions in Chestnut Hill. And at each stop, Lee asked the same ritual questions. She asked herself, or asked Harry. All the questions appeared on a ruled sheet of paper Mike had provided. Lee checked one box, left another blank, wrote in brief answers where they were called for, accumulating cryptic information, while Harry divided his attention between the map and the radio's constant conversation. The announcer was taking a trip to Hawaii, just he and as many of his close personal friends who paid a deposit before the end of the month. Harry was torn. Hawaii had always been the paradise of his dreams, hundreds or even thousands of dollars out of his reach. He longed to visit someplace as warm as Hawaii but didn't think he would enjoy traveling with a group. All breathing viruses on him, or germs.

The form Lee worked at was simple enough. In a column on the left of the page, in a sequence to which the map was keyed, was a series of names and addresses copied from Herb Calder's file of new Cadillac owners. Across the top of the page ran headings of the columns: Number of Cars Visible, Size of Garage (2-Car? 3-Car?), Any Children (Bikes? Toys?), and Owners Young or Old (List Evidence)?

The Sherman House on Emlen Street was scored as follows: "2 cars (Taurus & Cad.), 3-car garage; no kids (I think); maybe old people (rusty glider on porch and lace curtains)." Completing the form gave Lee a secondary interest. She tried to infer Mike's reasons for the strange questions. And so, though she and her father exchanged enough conversation to guide her on their twisting route through northwest Philadelphia, each of them had something more important to think about.

Harry pictured nut-brown maidens and felt warm, golden sand between his toes.

Lee found herself not only complying with Mike's requests—that was easy enough—but also making judgments he would depend upon, a kind of responsibility she didn't enjoy. Responsibility was not her thing, though this time she had to admit that there was something exciting about it, a treasure hunt. She secretly enjoyed the recent changes in Mike—feistiness, energy, vigor. She replayed in memory the feel of his back muscles in her hands, his breath in her ear, only hours ago. Her cheeks glowed and she daydreamed as she drove. Best of all, he needed her help. She recalled his face in slumber, hours before—a man she loved, a boy she could care for.

At the same time, Mike was busy completing Paulie's estate-planning sheet. His own lay finished and ready for Weiss' inspecting eye.

Shirley Frazee, an advocate of safe copying, refused to use the Xerox machine till the glass had been cleaned with alcohol.

Lester-the-thief supervised the manufacture of four pairs of Delaware license plates.

Theodore Winthrop boxed three rounds (fixed) with Tiger Guappo in his basement gym, his attention diverted by trying to understand the break-in at Colonial Cadillac. It didn't figure, a sure sign that it meant something important, and he considered the problem from several angles, a terrier harassing a treed squirrel or worrying a rat. It had to mean something. Until he knew what it meant, his imagination wouldn't drop it. He had to know, whether he ever used the knowledge or not.

He pinned Tiger's foot with his own and hit him a shot to the balls. Tiger went down. Theodore Winthop still felt unsatisfied. Tiger felt sore.

Paulie Klein had his own plans. His share of the proceeds from whatever it was he and Mike were doing would pay for engraved invitations to be sent to wallpaper company buyers and designers all over the East Coast. He would have the empty warehouse downstairs painted, better lights installed, contact a caterer about hors d'oeuvres and some liquor—a real blowout. And all for one reason: to stun the guests with Paul Joseph Klein originals hung on all four walls of the warehouse. There'd never been a sales pitch like it. He shivered with anticipation each time he thought of the boost it would give his career and that thought made him work even harder.

Meeting Lee had opened another exciting possibility. "Pick your best ten," she'd said. "I'll weave a two-by-three sample of each."

"Like a display book!"

"Only better," she promised. "Keep working on those samples and I'll set up the loom."

So Paulie plunged on. What he lacked in the way of equipment he made up for in labor and time. Thursday night he spent three hours cutting velvet crowns from a set of Goodwill used drapes, then gluing the crowns to strips of aluminum foil to be backed against butcher paper. A steam embossing press could do the job better, but by hand he could at least suggest the designs he had in mind. Involved in work he enjoyed, he let his cell phone ring a full three minutes before slamming down his scissors in disgust and snatching it off his belt to answer it. Some idiot wouldn't give up.

"What do you want?" he shouted into the phone. Maybe he could scare them off, since ignoring them did no good. It was Mike Bradley, asking that Paulie meet him. "Mike? Where are you?"

"In a phone booth two blocks up Washington. I pounded on the warehouse door for ten minutes. I could see your light on, so when you didn't come down I took a chance on calling you, but I don't want the cab driver to see where you live. Come up Washington to the first bar on your left, and bring along whatever you use to hot-wire an ignition."

"I'm working! You told me we were set till tomorrow night."

"My fault, Paulie. I thought the Flyers played tomorrow, but it's tonight. It's got to be now." Mike hung up. Wondering what hockey had to do with Lester-the-thief, Paulie walked past his sketchpad on the way out.

Mike held the cab door open and shook his head in warning. "Don't ask. Just get in," he said.

The cabby was curious when he dropped them at the arena. "You know you missed most of the action."

"That's okay," Mike told him. "If it's close enough, all that counts is the last two minutes."

"At ten bucks a minute? Have it your way." The cab drove off.

And Paulie let the dam burst. "Why tonight? You said nothing was going down till tomorrow. I've got my own work to do. I can't chase off like this in the middle of everything. Do you know how long it takes to heat-dry glued velvet? And what's so important about—"

"Wait," Mike said, leading Paulie toward The Spectrum exit ramp nearest them. "With any luck we... Here they come!"

Five shouting teenagers burst from the circular sports arena and sprinted down the exit ramp toward the parking lot. Behind them a few older men came trotting out of the building, wafted on the gush of warm, beery air that belched from all the opened doors. Paulie and Mike could see ten running figures, then thirty, then a steady stream of backlit silhouetted heads bobbing like a stampede coming at them out of the sunset. Mike pulled Paulie into the herd and they were swept along.

Mike talked as they kept pace with the crowd. "I did some checking after work, final details you might say, and we've got to walk down Packer Avenue to the big truck depot. If someone saw two of us on foot late at night, he'd wonder. This way we trail along with the hockey fans who parked there for the game."

"But, we could use your car. Why'd you buy the thing, if all we do is take the subway or walk?"

They stepped into the gutter to avoid the charge of three boisterous drunks playing tag through the thinning crowd on the sidewalk. "Lee's got the car. And you and I won't need it. Now, are you asking me for details?"

"I guess not, only it's happening so fast I'm not sure. Hey!" Paulie stopped at finding himself alone. He spun around and saw Mike a few strides behind him, standing still in the flow of people and watching him. Hurrying back, Paulie said, "What's wrong?"

"Too fast? Is it going too fast for you?"

"Awww, man, I didn't mean that. It's just, well . . . I've got a lot on my mind."

"I could tell. Tonight's the first time I've seen you without that sketchpad of yours."

"Jesus!" Paulie whirled and started back toward the warehouse. "I dropped it!"

"No, no, no. Calm down. You didn't have it when you got in the cab."

Paulie sighed. "Now, see? There you are. I'm so screwed up I'm forgetting things. . . . Is this going to take long? I should go back and get—"

"Not that long, if you're still sure." Mike put his hands on Paulie's shoulder to stop him and look him in the eye. "Give it to me straight. If you're having second thoughts—"

"Nothing like that. Hell, if your plans don't work, mine don't mean anything either. So, I'm with you, only we've got to get back quick while my glue's still hot."

Hugging Paulie around the neck with one arm, Mike urged him back into the flow of the crowd. "Quick as we can," he said. "Lee's meeting us at your place."

"Lee is? But why? Is she . . . ?" And then Paulie laughed at himself. "Okay, okay. I don't want to know."

Mike grinned and led the way.

Every few yards people dropped out of the moving crowd, some to enter gates to the parking lot, others to dart their suicidal way through snarling traffic on Packer Avenue to the bus stop across the street. Soon it wasn't a crowd but a drift of isolated groups, two or three animated fans chattering, each group wafting on its own scent: Kools, Liz Taylor White Diamonds, or Coors. The Flyers had won their second straight and the more optimistic were talking about the Stanley Cup playoffs months away. Some were fathers with small children unable to match the pace of the sprinters, here and there a young couple more interested in their mobile necking, or in the making out they had ahead of them than in the game they had just left. The night was clear, the air crisp enough to let breath hang misted in the light from the high pressure sodium lamps overhead; and the headlights of passing cars were turned a fog-lamp yellow, the sidewalk tinged peach by the fruit-gum glow of those lamps.

At the end of the third block Mike jerked his head aside and led Paulie off Packer down Lawrence. He stopped in mid-block. "Here we are," he said. "Can you hot-wire one of those?" A long row of trucks sat parked off Lawrence in a block-square muddy lot.

"I guess so. Why?"

"Let's do it."

They looked both directions to reassure themselves that no one was near, then crossed the matted, frost-killed grass, following muddy ruts to the row of trucks facing the street. In the semi-darkness they might have been visiting a Stephen King graveyard—ungainly monsters looming against the night sky, dinosaurs and their cubs, sprawled and spraddled in an indistinct corral.

"Why do you want . . . ?" Paulie let his own question die as he looked past the cabs to the trailers behind them. Though many were simple semi-trailers, milk trucks, moving vans parked for the night between deliveries, with here-and-there a battered and dented bus in their midst, the row to which Mike led the way was different. Not semi-trailers or vans, but car carriers. Sixty- and seventy-foot long complications of hydraulic and mechanical power, they squatted in a long row on multi-wheeled haunches.

"That's right," Mike said with a grin. "Car carriers. Now do your stuff." He pointed at a green White-GMC cab, linked to the orange mechanical geometry that would hold its load of new cars. It was empty, now.

"But where do we take it? Even after we start the thing, where do you take something as big as that mother. . . . Uh-huh. To my place, right?"

"You got it, Paulie. Your place. A nice, empty warehouse."

"When did you decide that?"

"Monday night. Does it matter?"

"I guess not." He scanned the row of trucks. "We've got to find one that's not locked."

"Locked?" Mike said. "Why? Who'd want to steal an empty car carrier?"

"Nobody I know." Paulie nodded sardonic agreement to the question. "Still, we better—"

"The first three aren't locked, I know. I checked them on the way home this afternoon."

"You checked them this afternoon. You walked up in daylight and tried the doors on three trucks while the drivers could have been somewhere here on the lot." Paulie stopped to think that over. "Yeah, I'll bet you did.

You know, sometimes you scare the hell out of me." He trotted through the dark field to clamber up into the cab of the first truck.

Mike climbed the other side. Inside the cab he took the flashlight Paulie waved in front of him. "There's no seat for me," he said.

Paulie nodded, distracted by the complexity of the dashboard. He bounced in the spring-mounted driver's seat. "No passengers," he muttered. "Flip over the milk crate."

Dumping a pile of rags and small tools from a plastic milk crate on the floor of the cab, Mike upended the crate and made himself a seat. He trained his flashlight on the dashboard. He watched Paulie duck under the steering wheel and come up with three wires in his hands.

"No sweat," Paulie whispered. "I twist these together and we go."

Mike shaded the flashlight with one hand and trained it on the wires. Paulie peeled back the insulation. He joined a pair of them, and the dashboard lights and gauges flared to life.

"Wait!" Mike whispered. "Hold it!"

Paulie dropped to the floorboards, banging his head on the hand brake. "What's the matter?" His voice quavered, his eyes shone white in the faint glow of the shaded flashlight.

"Before you start the engine, there's no gas."

"No what?"

"Take a look." Mike reached over to tap a pair of lighted fuel gauges, both registering less than a quarter full.

Paulie dragged himself back up onto the seat. "Gas! You want a truck with full tanks? You know, you're real picky for a guy who's stealing this rig."

"Do you want to drive into a station and tell them to fill it up? How much gas does this monster hold?"

"Maybe forty gallons in each tank."

"Besides questions to answer at the gas station. So, no gas, no deal. Let's try the next one."

"Okay, but if you bitch about the color or something, it's all off. I don't feature spending the rest of the night out here."

Flashlight off, Mike dropped from the cab and Paulie followed, leaving the door ajar behind them rather than slamming it. The truck next in line was another White-GMC hitched to the same trailer configuration as all the Mercedes and Volvo cabs parked beyond it.

"I know, don't tell me. It's unlocked," Paulie muttered, climbing into the cab. This time he bitched as he worked, not loud enough to be understood but loud enough to convey his feelings. He was not having fun. The connection made, he sat up. "Will this one suit you?"

"Love it," Mike told him. "Look." The fuel gauges both read full. "Can you drive one of these?"

"Why not? It's got a Spicer seven-gear transmission," Paulie said, pointing at a transmission diagram painted on a steel plate riveted to the driver's door above the window. He shifted several times, saying "I drove an old milk tanker once, with a Spicer-nine, before power steering and all that shit. I don't see reverse right off but it's got to be in here some place. Yeah, I can drive it."

"Okay, show me how."

"Why you? Why don't I just . . . ? Sorry. Never mind, or we'll be here another hour. Watch." Paulie settled himself behind the large wheel, and he shifted through the gears, explaining double-clutching to Mike. "Probably don't need to double-clutch the thing, if it's got a vacuum assist," he said. "But just in case. . . ." He located headlights, wiper switch, dimmer for the Christmas tree of lights on the cab and along the base of the trailer. "Now, you happy? Can we go?"

"One more thing."

"Oh, Jesus!" Paulie wiped his sweating face with his hands, then scrubbed his palms along his thighs to dry them. "What is it?"

"I see how this one works. Crawl over and hot-wire the next one, will you?"

"The next one." It was a statement, not a question, and Paulie's tone implied that he might never again ask a question as long as he lived. "This truck is okay, you just said, so you want me to start a different one."

"Not a 'different' one. Another one, and you drive it. I'll take this one."

There was a long silence in the cab. Seated where they were, five feet above the ground staring out at a row of trucks facing them, a dark field around them lighted at the edges by the bobbing lights of passing traffic, Paulie Klein felt a calm isolation. In a moment they would leave, and his heart would start climbing into his throat, as it had at Colonial Cadillac. But for now he felt a sense of peace. If only he could sit still where he was. . . . Nothing Mike could say would shake his serenity, nothing would surprise him. He vowed that. A long pause let him frame what he swore was his last question, at least till they were safely in the warehouse. "Mike, I trust you, you know that. I know you've got everything figured out, and like that. And I don't want you to take this wrong. I'm almost afraid to ask, you know what I mean? Because, if you're thinking what I think you're thinking . . . Well, you know what I mean."

Mike nodded.

"Okay, then. I just want to know. You're going to drive this rig back to my place, even though you never drove a semi before."

"Uh-huh."

"Right.... And you want me to start another one. You also want me to...uh...to drive it home? Besides the one you're driving home?"

"Uh-huh."

"Because...?" The word lasted four seconds.

"Because I found out today these things can carry a dozen Hondas apiece but only ten Cadillacs or Lincolns." Mike drew upon the image growing clearer each moment in mind, a picture that implied power and success and wealth all at once, himself and Lee and Paulie driving into the Pine Barrens in a thundering parade. "Saturday night, we're taking twenty new Caddies to Lester-the-thief."

"Twenty of 'em."

"Uh-huh."

Paulie blinked. "Twenty of 'em?"

"Uh-huh."

Shaking his head, he opened the cab door and slid to the ground. "Son of a bitch! Twenty of 'em!"

It was 11:30, the streets quiet and the Flyers fans well homeward bound when Mike led the way out of the semi-trailer parking area off Lawrence Street. He pulled forward, stalled twice on the rutted field as the cold engine killed, but by the time he restarted its thundering diesel and bounced the empty, rattling, seventy-five-foot carrier down over the curb onto 7th Street he had the feel of it. Paulie followed him out Oregon to Delaware Avenue, then north toward Washington. They criss-crossed the train tracks running down Delaware, jolted through potholes, passed ranks of parked trucks, trailers, and railroad cars shunted onto a siding for unloading. The traffic here was sparse and trucks a common sight. Still, out of caution, Paulie kept a full block behind Mike so they wouldn't be seen running together. He was torn between the urge to pass Mike's dawdling truck and the fear that they were already going too fast. Some cop might notice them bouncing and rattling along the quiet street at 35 MPH and decide to ticket them.

Approaching the warehouse, Mike blinked his lights twice and smiled to see the large doors tilt up and disappear, each door running back on its overhead track. Lee stood in the shadows beside the door switch, big-eyed, as Mike's truck jolted over the threshold and rolled to within five feet of the far wall before stopping. Mike separated the ignition wires and dropped to the floor in time to watch Paulie lumber in behind him. Paulie's truck stopped. The giant doors purred shut.

Without a word Paulie jumped from the White-GMC cab and dashed up the stairs to his loft apartment.

"Where's he going?" Lee asked. "Something wrong?"

"He'll be back. Did you bring the other stuff?"

"Right here." She showed him cans of paint, stencils, masking tape, a pair of small brushes, all organized and displayed across the bottom of an upended orange crate.

Paulie found his sketchpad where he'd left it on the floor. He tucked it under his arm and walked back down to the warehouse, stopping on the stairway landing to take a comforting deep breath. All safe and secure. He was home. The lights were on. Mike had finished applying a square frame of masking tape around the company name on the cab door and stepped back while Lee, shaking a spray can of black paint, took his place.

"Come give us a hand," Mike said. His voice sounded flat and distant in the huge room. "We've got four doors to repaint before we can quit tonight."

Paulie cantered down the staircase and walked straight to Lee. "Did he"—a jerk of his head indicated Mike at work on the second truck—"did he tell you why we brought two of them?"

Shaking her head, Lee said, "I thought in case something goes wrong with the first one. He's careful like that. He alphabetizes and recopies his shopping lists."

"Twenty cars! We're taking twenty Caddies out to Lester." He nodded, pleased at the shocked look his information drew.

"Mike? Is that right?"

"That's right, Babe.... O.K., the door's masked. Ready to spray."

Lee dropped the spray can to the floor and folded her arms. "I went along with you this far, but you've got to do some explaining. This whole thing's getting out of hand. I never bargained for something this big. You said a quiet, little—"

"You did say that," Paulie interrupted to join the accusation. "Just a simple—"

"Okay." Mike shrugged. "And I meant it. Look, everything I've read claims that the big theft is the one that works. Something daring, bold—what the newspapers like to call 'daylight' and 'clever' and all those headline words. They say the big caper is the one that succeeds. I don't believe it."

"Great! You don't believe it," Lee said. "So you're stealing twenty cars. Nothing big, noth—"

"Hey, now, will you listen?" Mike motioned them to a bench at the side wall, and when they sat he ticked off items on his fingers. "If we went out to blow the Franklin Mint, or say we hijacked an armored car, that's big trouble, agreed?"

They nodded, all attentiveness.

"But one thing the cops don't get worried about is the little job. I know, remember? Lester took our Honda, and the cops couldn't be bothered. What's one car theft? Peanuts. Now, if we backed up to Colonial and loaded twenty Cadillacs at once on these rigs, we'd have the cops, and FBI, and every string band in South Philadelphia out hunting for us."

"That's what we're saying!" Lee looked to Paulie for confirmation and got his vehement nod. "Twenty is—"

"You're not listening, Babe. We won't steal twenty cars, that's the wrong way to think of it. We're amateurs, small time and going to stay that way. All I want to do is take one car, one Cadillac, twenty different times. There's a big difference. Nobody will connect twenty different... 'misplaced' cars, even if they hear about all of them, and I don't plan for that to happen. Before anyone knows we've touched even one Caddy, we'll be sitting right here, counting Lester's money, all safe and clear."

"That's it, isn't it?" Lee asked, in tune with Mike's real intention. "It's *Lester's* money you want, not just money."

"Part of the fun," Mike said. "And imagine the look on his face when we drive up not with one, or two, or three, but twenty new Cadillacs! No one's ever done it before. And Lester can eat a little crow."

Neither Paulie nor Lee looked convinced, but they listened. Lee was the first to think of an objection. "All we do is run errands. How do we know your plan's going to work?"

"Ahhh, that's where you trust me, the same as I'm trusting you. . . . Paulie? Did I ask you to prove to me you could hot-wire these car carriers?"

"No, but—"

"Damn right, no! You said you could, I took your word for it, and it worked. Everybody's contributing—Paulie here, with lots of experience I don't pretend to have. Practical things, like the contact with Lester, getting past a live burglar alarm. I'd be up the creek trying any of that myself. And Lee, you always anchor my fantasies. If I go too far, it's up to you to stop me."

"Or try," she said.

"Or try. And you can gather tools and materials they'll never connect with two men, in case anyone ever looks close enough at Paulie or me to get a description. Even Harry, whether he knows it or not, he's got a part to play. We're all in this together."

"But you're not telling us all of it!" Lee protested.

"I'm telling you what you have to know, when you have to know it. That's my contribution. The plan stays right here." He tapped his forehead. "Alternatives, contingencies, I promise you it'll work. I don't question your contribution, and you can't ask me for details. If nobody else knows, there can't be a leak. What it all comes down to is, do you trust me?"

Lee looked hurt at the question. "I love you," she said.

"I hope that's the same thing." Mike looked to Paulie, and waited. "Well? We can still call it off."

Snorting, Paulie threw up his hands. "And what? Take these back where we got them? That'd be worse than taking them, in the first place. Not me, man. I don't set foot out of here till daylight. Long as we're done for today, I'm in."

"Better than that," Mike told them. "We're clear till Saturday morning. Then Harry joins us."

"Daddy? I don't know, Mike. He won't like it. When we went out today he was pretty cranky about it."

"Did you bring the survey with you?"

"It's over there." Lee pointed at her jacket and handbag lying atop a tablet at the foot of the wooden staircase.

"Then, let's get a coat of paint on those truck doors, and I'll go through it with both of you. Harry won't mind when he hears. His part's easy." Mike walked away, much less certain than he made himself sound. He could hear his own footsteps on the concrete floor. Now was the time. If either Lee or Paulie backed out now, he could still call it off. But if they came along...

Saturday was getting closer.

He waited.

A scraping noise almost drew his head around but he steeled himself not to look. Then there were footsteps as Lee trotted past with the spray can in her hand. "I'll get this one," she said.

"Do you want anything but the doors masked?" Paulie's voice came from behind him.

And Mike relaxed. "No. People don't read all those permit numbers on the trailer anyway. Just the doors." He made a mental note: stage three, coming up.

Sitting on wooden chairs in Paulie's apartment, Lee picked at black paint dried under the nail of her forefinger, Paulie doodled on his sketchpad. They reviewed Lee's pledge to weave a sample book of "woolen wallpaper" for Paulie's show but also watched Mike pore over the survey and map Lee had brought with her. He made a few check marks, went through the list another time—his fourth—and rolled onto his back to look up at them.

"Got them," he said. "Twenty targets, and four alternates just in case."

Paulie and Lee hiked their chairs closer. Mike swung his long legs around to sit cross-legged and hold up the map for them to see. Twenty stars dotted the map, and four small circles.

"Each of these families"—his finger tapped the starred locations—"has at least two cars. They're less likely to miss one of them right away." He smiled and waved away Lee's unvoiced protest. "You wanted to know, so I'm telling you. Part of it. You'll see what I mean. Anyway, they do have transportation and can spare the new car, if they have to. A one-car family couldn't.

"Most of them have no little kids, as far as you could tell, right?"

Lee nodded.

"Another reason to keep them on the list. Kids are sharp and ask too many questions. They see details a busy adult's likely to overlook.

"Some of the ones I picked out could have a gardener or a cleaning woman, at least their houses are big enough; and it's important we deal with people used to being catered to, people who don't handle their own little domestic chores.

"And last, none of them lives on a one-way street where we might get bottled in, if we have to cut and run."

"Run?" Paulie stiffened. "You said there was no danger."

"There's not, but we'd be stupid to ignore the possibility." He nodded to them. "We're ready. Harry and I will pick you up here at nine Saturday morning." He looked at Lee. "That's Harry's job, doing some driving for us, that's all.

"I can drive."

"You'll be busy, right . . . " His pencil point roved over the map before settling. "Right here. Three phone booths in front of a Wal-Mart store. No one's going to get shook if you keep one of the three tied up most of the day."

Lee poked Paulie to get his attention before she asked Mike, "Would it do me any good to ask why I'll be in the phone booth?"

"Making phone calls."

Paulie said. "It won't do you any good."

"I mean, why not call from here? Use my cell phone?"

"And have it traced?"

"Okay," Lee said. "I get it. . . . Tomorrow I'll go get some change."

Mike winked at her. "There's a roll of quarters in our top dresser drawer, and a roll of dimes. I picked them up yesterday." He laughed when she stuck out her tongue at him. "Paulie?"

Paulie shook his head. "Nope. I'm through with the questions. You pick me up Saturday morning."

"Wear your coveralls and a cap to cover your hair. Now," Mike stood and said, "are you two ready to name our new truck company? The paint should be dry enough to stencil over it. Any ideas?"

"How about Heritage Old-Line Fidelity Trucking Company?" Paulie asked.

Lee smiled. "We could call it 'Keep on Truckin.'"

Mike said, "Maybe we'd better call it 'A-1.' It takes less paint."

"Awww, damn!" Paulie said. "Everybody's called A-1 something or other."

"Uh-huh. That's another reason."

SATURDAY

Saturday morning was bright and crisp, after the second heavy frost of the fall. No more heat waves, no more gummy humidity till spring. The air was invigorating and a clear sign that a new season had settled on Philadelphia—pumpkins ripening in Bucks County, mink coats swaddling the languid mannequins in Lord and Taylor's window. Roads pointed north were filled with families setting out to survey the gold and umber glow of Pocono forests. Early shoppers on their way into Center City smiled at one another, and a man on the Red Arrow trolley from Media to 69th Street offered his seat to a woman who wasn't pregnant. A new day had dawned.

For Theodore Winthrop, Saturday meant an hour's sculling on the Schuylkill River, followed by a late-morning business meeting and a late-afternoon helicopter trip to New York for the theater that night. His wife loved big, splashy musicals. He loved his wife, and he could sleep through all that caterwauling onstage.

King Kolchak thought it was Sunday. He planned a day of TV-watching. He didn't consider attending the

Eagles' game, though his wallet held four thirty-yard-line tickets that no one else wanted.

Lee Schaeffer settled herself in a phone booth outside Wal-Mart on Passyunk Avenue, two cartons of soy milk and a brown paper sack of carob-coated tofu bonbons between her feet, a list of Mike's neatly-printed instructions in her hand. She scanned her schedule again: twenty names and phone numbers to call, each at a specific time, and four alternates. She held a handwritten speech to read to each person she contacted, and Mike's most serious warning at the bottom of the page in block capitals: "ANSWER INCOMING CALLS, 'COLONIAL CADILLAC, MISS WEBSTER SPEAKING.'" Mike might ask someone to call her, or might phone to tell her to cut and run, if for some reason the plan began to come apart.

Other than those tasks, she had nothing to do but to sit and wait. She sat with her back turned to passersby, thumbed her sunglasses tight to the bridge of her nose, and opened the Honda owner's manual. Great stuff! Even a schematic of the electrical system!

Friday Paulie and Mike had sweated through their final exam at Heritage. Though the fifteen new trainees wouldn't know the results till the award ceremony Monday morning in the Heritage Building conference room, this Saturday morning, Carleton Weiss sat grading the exams, and he knew: Mike Bradley was first in his class, with Paulie Klein a surprising fourteenth, subceded at the bottom of the list only by Robert Boyle, who didn't understand what was expected of him. Weiss gave Esther Flett a "zero" and passed her without reading the exam, assuming that it was beyond her competence. As far as Weiss was concerned, she had a job locked up—Heritage Old Line Fidelity Token-of-the-Week. But as an afterthought he read her exam answers and found them flawless, in his mind the result of cheating. No other possibility.

Mike and Harry arrived at Paulie's apartment at 9:00 AM. Paulie trotted out to slip into the Honda, where he donned a black handlebar mustache Mike handed him. Mike's was in place, auburn-brown, and looked real enough to fool everyone but Harry. On principle Harry, sitting cramped in the backseat, found it fake and childish. They headed west toward the first stop of the day.

Lois Enright had dreamt about this Saturday for months. But since Friday noon the day had threatened to turn into a nightmare. The number of crises she faced would have staggered anyone with less grit. That was one trait Lois Enright had in quantity; no one a mere thirty-seven gets elected social chairman of the Friends of Versailles without grit, determination, drive, and the willingness and ability to buy votes. Lois had been elected. Tonight would pay off some of her debts, as well as squelching the bastards who'd voted against her. A dinner party—call it *the* dinner party—for a select sixty people, some from Wilmington, Delaware; Washington, DC; Westbury, Connecticut; a few Philadelphians of course (one of them sister-in-law to a Biddle), and the DesRosiers from Chevy Chase. Nothing could shake her on this day of days, not even the string of disasters she had already withstood.

The cleaning woman had refused to come on Friday. Lois found where the vacuum cleaner was kept and used it, herself. Then that moron of a caterer—no beluga caviar, only some Romanian trash (though he did promise beluga labels embossed at the bottom of each container). Her husband Fred was trapped in Denver by a blizzard and would be late, if he made the party at all. Jerry Long could fill in as host, as he had filled in for Fred on several bedsheet-rumpling weekends with Lois at the Marriott. Lois ticked off her list of substitutions and ground her teeth.

One bright spot lit her otherwise dismal morning: the Queen Anne mirror over the Delft-tiled fireplace offered Lois a vision of herself, little marred by the authentic tarnish in the mirror. Lois Enright was beautiful. At thirty-seven she looked twenty-nine. Well, thirty. From her perfect (capped) teeth and pert nose (a bargain at $6850 in Lausanne) to the soft wave of her natural (looking) auburn hair ($175 plus tip that very morning, in the small upstairs sitting room, by Mister Stephen himself), she was the picture of unretouched womanhood—a thought she held as she went to phone the caterer again.

The telephone startled her by ringing as she reached for it. For a moment she debated ignoring the flashing button and using one of the other lines, but it might be a guest calling. With a well-founded sense of foreboding, she took the call. Herself. That was yet another crisis: she had to answer her own phone! Forbes had laryngitis. "Yes?" she sang.

What she heard was a brassy, nasal screech, one of these awful Philadelphia accents, reciting, "Mrs. Enright? This is Miss Webster at Colonial Cadillac. Our records show that last month your husband bought a car from us, license number—"

"I'm sure I don't know the number, dear. What's this about?"

"You may have read, Mrs. Enright, about a malfunction in the brake system of the new Sedan de Villes. It was in the papers. That Nader man discovered it. Ralph Nader."

Lois bit a nail without thinking, then looked in horror at the damage and snapped, "Is he still doing that?"

"We're recalling all Sedan de Villes for immediate repairs, Mrs. Enright. There's a man on his way out to your house right now. If you'll give him the keys and the title, we'll perform the repairs, record that fact on your title, and return the car to you Monday morning."

"Listen, Miss.... What was your name again?"

"Webster. Julia Webster," Lee read from her script. "Do you wish to phone me back at this number and authenticate this call?"

"Why would I...? Never mind all that. Must these repairs of yours be done this very—"

"Our man is on his way now, Mrs. Enright. The keys, and the title, and we're sorry to trouble you."

"Oh, all right! Tell him to come to the back door." Lois considered slamming down the phone to show her displeasure but decided that would be common. Instead she grew saccharine. "Thank you so very much, dear." She hung up and made a face. "Shit!"

Halfway through dialing the caterer she was interrupted by the front doorbell. "Forbes!" she called out, in her most ladylike shout, then whispered "Goddamnit!" and went to answer the door.

A young man stood there, broad shoulders, a mustache the color of her own auburn hair. She started to close the door on him but stopped as she noticed his uniform: gray coveralls labeled "Colonial Cadillac" over the breast pocket.

"Hello," he said, bewilderment in his voice. "Does a. . . . " He looked at a card in his hand. "Does a Mrs. Enright live here?"

"I'm Lois Enright."

"Oh, sorry. I didn't expect someone so . . . " His voice trailed off behind the first blush Lois had seen in months. His compliment was stronger unspoken, and she was spared the problem of responding to it.

A nice touch, Mike congratulated himself, as he saw her smile and relax her grip on the door.

"You're here for the car," she told him. "If you'll wait, I'll get the keys. They're in my bedroom." She walked away half-angry at herself for saying that, half-smiling at what she'd heard in the word "bedroom," even on such a busy day as this. Oh well, Fred wasn't that old, and if Fred didn't get back from Denver by dinnertime, Jerry Long could stay on an hour or so after the others left.

Mike eased inside the door. He didn't want to stand any longer than necessary where a curious neighbor could see him, even though the Enright house was well back from the shaded street. He admired the entry hall; these people could buy a dozen new cars without denting their bank account. The situation seemed right. And looked good, he told himself, as he watched Lois Enright's ankles, then calves come into sight down the stairs.

She said something about a servant being ill—he didn't catch it—and handed him the keys and title. Her hand was cool, her eyes challenged him to test her temperature elsewhere. He let his hand hold hers longer than he should have, long enough that she had the satisfaction of pulling away. Now she'd romanticize him as a type, rather than remembering him, that poor young man she'd had to send off.

"Thank you, Mrs. Enright. And, the car?"

"In back. In the garage. I'm rather busy this morning, so you won't mind if I don't show you the way."

"Of course. We'll have the car back Monday." As the door closed, he added, "I may bring it myself." Let her chew on that one.

Whistling, he circled the house to find the garage, a wing in itself with five separate doors. It took only moments to slip on his rubber gloves, start the car—a midnight blue Sedan de Ville, resplendent in its waxed and gleaming beauty—and guide it out the sweeping drive past the other side of the house to the street. The car purred, and floated, not as tight-sprung and abrupt as the Honda. Mike turned on WHYY and let the car's multi-speaker stereo bathe him in Dvorak's *New World Symphony.* Life was good.

"I used to think Mike was a good influence on Lee, but anymore I don't know." Harry Schaeffer grumbled as he sat hunched over the wheel of the Honda. His monologue had gone on ever since they'd dropped Mike at the corner and driven past the Enright address, though Paulie listened to little of it.

"What's keeping him?" Paulie craned his neck to peer at the Enright house.

"A man in my condition's got to think of things like that. Who'll look after Lee when I'm gone?"

"Yes, I see what you mean.... Listen. Do you think we should just sit here? What if he... Here he comes!"

Harry jerked around to watch a midnight blue Cadillac cruising toward them. It passed, and the driver nodded. His auburn moustache dropped loose at one end and dangled.

"That's it!" Paulie whooped. "He pulled it off. I knew he could." His eyes grew round. "That makes it my turn." He tugged a baseball cap lower to cover his curly hair and nodded. "I guess I gotta try it."

Harry pulled away from the curb. "It's not knowing is what's the bad part. I mean, if you're allergict to something, there's got to be something you're allergict to."

"Hortter and Greene Streets," Paulie reminded him. "Some people named Winkler, and we don't want to get behind schedule."

"Do you know what it's like to go through life not knowing?"

"What?" Paulie stared at him as if seeing Harry for the first time. "What are you talking about?"

"It's not cats or dogs, or any food I could name, though come to think of it I do belch tomatoes for a couple days after."

"Harry? My uncle's an allergist. Next week I'll get you an appointment, okay?"

"I'm not sure it will do any good. Experts have tried to—"

"But till then, can you shut up and drive? Hortter and Greene. Winkler."

Harry coughed once, for practice, but drove on.

The Winkler house hadn't been painted in fifteen years. Weeds choked the yard, waist-high, gone to seed and frost-killed brown. There were two Cadillacs in the drive, one still bearing the delivery slip in the left rear window. Paulie walked up the brick sidewalk to the front porch, counting the steps. He would have to return the same way. He rehearsed his speech and went over Mike's warnings. If for some reason Lee hadn't got through on the phone, Paulie was to explain his mission, then give them the number of Lee's phone and tell Winkler to call for confirmation. And if the Winklers seemed at all suspicious, he would offer to come back on Monday, then get the hell out.

The front door loomed. He didn't feel ready; but then he doubted that he'd ever feel ready. He raised a hand to knock, when the front door flew open. An old man, coatless and wearing sleeve garters, both a belt and suspenders (crazy, what things you notice, Paulie thought) stepped out and closed the door behind him. He held out a set of car keys and an envelope.

"Here, take them, but I want you to know one thing. There was a time when the name 'Cadillac' meant quality. That's all I've got to say."

Paulie felt cheated. He hadn't spoken a word, all his rehearsals wasted. He cleared his throat to thank the man.

"Oh, another thing. If I don't miss my guess, you get paid by the hour. Is that a fact?"

"Uhhh." Paulie nodded.

"And you stand around like this. I saw the way you dawdled up my sidewalk. It's no wonder repair bills are so outrageous. If I get charged one penny for this brake job, I'll take it right straight to the Better Business Bureau, understand?"

"Uhh, yes sir."

"See that you do!" The door closed in Paulie's face.

"Do what?" Paulie turned on his heel and fell off the porch. Dried rosebushes snagged at his overalls and held him for a moment but he snatched free and stumbled across the weed-filled yard to the nearer car. He fumbled at the door to unlock it. A window opened behind him and the man shouted, "It's not locked! Are you sure you can drive that car without wrecking it?"

Paulie nodded.

"See that you do." The window slammed down.

Paulie managed to stay on the driveway and backed into traffic. He swung around and drove past Harry on the corner where he beeped the horn—a discreet, mellow three-toned chord suited both to the gray Caddy and to the sedate neighborhood—and watched Harry fall in line to follow him back to the warehouse.

Mike was waiting, his Sedan de Ville nose-to-tail behind a car carrier whose loading ramps had been dropped to the floor. Between them he and Paulie got both cars jockeyed aboard in ten minutes. They parked them atop the cab and secured each with four safety chains already dangling in place from the car carrier's loading treads.

"We'll load the next couple faster," Mike promised, "now that we see how it works. Ready?"

Paulie nodded. They climbed into the Honda and started out again.

"How'd it go?" Mike asked.

"Piece of cake."

They both laughed, to Harry's visible disgust, and Mike checked his watch. The time was 9:44. In one minute Lee would make her second set of phone calls. On schedule.

"Should have seen me," Paulie said. "I walked up there, grabbed the keys right out of Winkler's hand, and drove off. Hell, this is so easy, I should have thought of it myself."

"Sure," Harry said. "Easy. Now tell him how you fell into Winkler's flower bushes."

"Only once!" Paulie assured Mike. "And it didn't matter, did it? I got the car."

"You got it."

All the way back to Chestnut Hill, Mike and Paulie traded smug grins.

At 5:20, a full hour later than planned, Mike dropped the pins into the locking bar on the second loaded car carrier and stepped back to admire his work. Done. Now the delay didn't matter any longer, though during the confusion that caused it he had grown edgy enough to snap at Paulie, a lapse he regretted, showing Paulie his state of nerves. It all stemmed from the weather. The day was too pleasant; people were out riding, shopping, or for one reason or another not home on this lazy Saturday, and Lee had been forced to go to the alternates on her list. That meant a series of hurried calls by Mike from booths scattered along Harry's preplanned route, last minute changes of destination, and delay.

Now that it was over, the delay seemed more rewarding than troublesome. It proved Mike's foresight in picking alternates, and the right number of them at that, a happy accident he couldn't have predicted. Twenty-four names on the final list, compiled from Herb Calder's files at Colonial Cadillac, twenty new cars sitting before him now in gleaming, expensive, negotiable beauty. And of the twenty owners visited only two had been uncooperative, at first—neither of them so much suspicious as irritated at having a new car reclaimed on such short notice. With them, as with everyone else, the name "Ralph Nader" had resolved all doubts. The next time the aging Nader ran for president—and he would, he would—Mike might even vote for him instead of writing in Harold Stassen.

The moment Mike and Paulie had the last car loaded in place they changed clothes. Paulie was up in his apartment, with a razor blade shredding the gray coveralls to make them easier to burn. He and Mike wore jeans and sweatshirts in their stead. Lee was home, Harry on his way there. Only two more steps remained to complete the day's work—a final phone call to Lester-the-thief, and a nap scheduled for Mike and Paulie, 6:00 till 9:00, when Lee would arrive at the warehouse with their dinner.

A satisfying achievement. Like assembling a three dimensional jigsaw puzzle. One piece, then a second and third, all of them balanced against one another till a key block slipped home to tie the construct together, tidy, perfected, a seamless unit.

Mike checked the large warehouse doors once more. Locked tight. He walked upstairs to congratulate Paulie.

The trio enjoyed a picnic atop an old stadium blanket spread on the concrete floor of the warehouse. "Ham and cheese without the ham," Mike said, helping Lee to lay out the feast she'd brought for them.

"What's that mean?" Paulie said, lifting one piece of bread to peer at the ham-less ham sandwich.

"Hers is cheeseless, too," Mike said.

"Vegemite," Lee said. "Don't pay any attention to Mike." She leaned over to kiss his cheek.

Paulie asked, "What's this hairy stuff?"

"You've seen sprouts before," Lee said.

"Not in my food!"

Mike bit into his sandwich as if he enjoyed it, while Lee passed around a basket of fruit. "You can get used to anything."

Lights played off the cars and reflected colors more cheering than bright sunlight. The chill floor gave them an excuse for the shivers they might have felt anyway. It was a fine, giddy party. Mike basked in the glow of hero-worship Lee and Paulie directed his way, though he made a few half-hearted attempts to deny his brilliance. Half-hearted, because it was difficult not to feel a touch of that same admiration, less for himself than for the child of his labors: "the plan." He enjoyed hearing Paulie and Lee recount the complexities of it all and praise its perfect unfolding. The mental juggling required to implement his plan pleased him even more than the sight of the loaded car carriers. And the final delight to savor was Lester's disbelief on the phone.

"Did he say he'd have the money ready?" Lee persisted.

"He'll have it, though he doesn't think we'll claim it. What do you say? Ready to go surprise him?"

Paulie stuck his mustache in place, shouted "Geronimo!" and ran for his truck.

Their departure was chaos.

Mike had neglected to have them practice backing the car carriers, a task difficult enough with any large truck. "These suckers," Paulie shouted over the engine noise, "bend in the middle!" The car carriers were "hinged" to articulate not behind the cab like other semi-trailers but some twenty feet further back. The cab and four cars of the load comprised a front section, with six other cars loaded on the come-along rear unit. It took Mike five minutes to jockey his loaded rig back and forth till he cleared the doors. Paulie had a worse time of it. Twice he backed into the doorframe. But then he was free, outside, sweat-damp and cursing in the cab while Lee closed the double doors and ran to start the Honda.

They headed north up Delaware Avenue in spaced single file, Paulie leading, Mike a distant second, and Lee bringing up the rear. It was part of Mike's delivery plan, what he called "The Payoff: Stage Four." If anything happened to either of the trucks they would abandon it on the spot and Lee would pick up the driver to bring him along to Lester's. Mike couldn't imagine that circumstance, but they were too close now to final success for them to risk the trip into New Jersey without some contingency planning.

Mike's truck surprised him by demanding physical strength to handle it. Loaded, it felt unresponsive, and the large steering wheel shimmied in his hands at each pothole he crossed. His forearms were soon trembling and his shoulders grew stiff. At 11:00 PM there were few cars on the street, and fewer trucks. He concentrated on holding his lane and keeping the running lights of Paulie's rig in sight. Busy with the physical work of guiding the truck, he failed to notice the traffic light at Chestnut stop the truck ahead of him. He pulled up behind Paulie, exactly where he didn't want to be. No one would pay much attention to a single car carrier;

someone might be curious at seeing a pair of them nose-to-tail, loaded like a 150-foot train driving Philadelphia's otherwise empty streets late Saturday night.

But catching up to Paulie proved lucky. Seated there waiting for the light to turn green, he scanned Paulie's load and flinched at the problem he saw. The last car loaded atop the truck wasn't "new"; it bore a license plate! If he noticed it, someone else could. Tollbooth attendants saw loads like this coming through every day.

A glance in the mirror told him no one was behind them. He had to get those plates off, now, right here in the street. He gunned his truck out around Paulie and waved him to the curb, pulling to the side fifty yards past the light.

He was out and running as his car carrier coasted to a thumping stop against the high curb. He leapt onto the step atop the driver-side gas tank on Paulie's cab and shouted "License plates! Take them off!" In the same motion he scrambled up over the front fender and ladder, past Paulie's startled eyes, into the rank of Cadillacs on the top level.

Using a dime for a screwdriver, he worked the first plate free while Paulie was still trying to understand what was wrong. Mike waved Lee on past when she stopped the Honda beside them—that was all he needed, a traffic jam to call attention to their problem. When Paulie caught on and got to work, Mike ran back to his own rig to strip the plates from his ten cars, while he worked giving thanks that the State of Pennsylvania didn't require front plates as well as back. He collected Paulie's plates and his own, tossed them into the milk crate on the floor beside him in the truck cab where—in another vehicle—a passenger seat might be, and slid trembling behind the wheel.

Only ten minutes to unscrew the plates but his fingers were already cramped and sore; his clammy sweatshirt clung to his back. After a moment to calm himself, to dim the rig's Christmas tree and check in the rearview mirror for a responding blink of lights from Paulie, he set out again. He passed Lee. She fell in behind as they neared the approach ramp to the Ben Franklin Bridge across the Delaware River into New Jersey.

All the way across the bridge he held to the far-right lane and maintained a sedate 25 MPH. His imagination raced ahead over their route, trying to foresee other difficulties. How could he have overlooked something so obvious as those license plates? Not that it mattered, now. Resolved, the problem was unimportant but for the possibilities it contained. If Mike found himself shaken by it, what had it done to Paulie?

Paulie was exhilarated. He had walked the tightrope again without falling. Adrenaline made him light-headed and he sang, roaring out tuneless noises and pounding the steering wheel with the heel of his hand. This was more fun than riding The Whip, tension galore, like the last few seconds before orgasm. In his delight he considered passing Mike on the bridge and racing him to the tollgates. No, Mike wouldn't see the fun in that. Paulie sighted along his truck hood and imitated a machine gun with a few chattering verbal shots into Mike's rear tires.

And Lee rode snug in the cradling leather bucket seat of the Prelude, wrapped and protected and warm and secure, the dash lights a soft glow before her. The radio played oldies, the night was clear, and she could almost enjoy their collective success. A family, she thought—she and Harry and Mike, and now Paulie along with them. She hummed as the road swept under the car and trailed away behind her.

They all swung over the crest of the bridge and rolled downhill toward Jersey. The tollgates, four of them open, were spot-lighted oases in the darkness, displayed in distant perspective forced by the rows of bridge lights parallel above on each side and narrowing ahead to a funnel mouth. As he neared the tollgates Paulie surrendered to impulse and swung left around Mike's rig, headed for the only empty lane he could see. He pumped the hissing brakes and cranked down his window. In the box on the floor beside him in a Maxwell House coffee can were a twenty-dollar bill, a ten, a five, five ones and a dollar's worth of silver—another example of Mike's foresight. Whatever the toll for a truck this size might be, Mike had made certain that both he and Paulie would have exact change ready. No delays here, under the glare of lights.

Paulie hung an arm out his window and waited for the magic words.

The attendant stared at him.

"Okay, man, how much?"

"You ever cross this bridge before?"

"What? Look, I asked you how much." Something was wrong. Paulie's delight ebbed and he glanced in the pair of mirrors mounted on the cab's front fenders. Lee was pulling up to stop behind him.

The attendant folded his arms and feigned patience. He was not a good actor. "You miss the point, Jack. The point is, this lane's for official vehicles only. Y'see, there's a sign back there above you, got lights on it and everything, and that sign says 'Official Vehicles Only." That means passenger cars only. So back your ass outa here and get the hell over where you belong!"

"Back it . . . ?" Paulie checked again. There were two cars ranked behind him now. Even if he could back the truck—something he doubted after his two collisions with the warehouse door—he was blocked. "Listen, mister. I'm sorry, but you can see how it is. I can't back up with those cars back there. Let me pay you, and I'll—"

"Want me to lose my job?" Through some clever trick the red-faced attendant kept his voice low while he shouted. "I got my orders. No truck comes through this lane, and that means no truck. Not you, not nobody. So move it!"

"What's the trouble, Manny?" A uniformed state trooper walked into sight around the front of the toll-booth. "Anything I can do?"

Paulie pressed his mustache tighter and prayed for the bridge to collapse under them.

The attendant whirled around as if stung. "Does it look like it? Did I ask for your help? I've been working this bridge here three years, and I never asked for help yet, did I?" He turned back to Paulie. "Are you going to get that damn thing out of here, or do I call my supervisor?"

"He's right," the trooper said. "There's a sign back there. Maybe you didn't read it. 'Official Vehicles—.'"

"I already told him that," the attendant said. "We were getting along fine, till you horned in. Now you've got everybody watching, you and that damned uniform."

"Look, Manny." The trooper's face took on the color of spoiled beef, shading toward eggplant. "Don't give me any of your mouth. I've got a job to do, too, remember?"

"Please. I don't want you guys arguing over me," Paulie said. "So let me pay up and I'll—"

"You shut up and stay out of this!" the trooper yelled. "Unless you want a citation. You looking for trouble?"

Paulie shook his head. "Not me, officer."

Mike had seen Paulie pulling parallel with him, headed left into the wrong lane. There was nothing he could do about it, not while he fought his own truck to a stop, nothing at all. He paid a bored attendant and started away. A parking area on the right gave him a place to swing out of traffic and sit in anguished thought, trying to devise some way of rescuing Paulie without getting both of them nabbed. He slumped in his seat and peered at the rearview mirror. A tollbooth attendant and a state trooper argued about something, gesturing in anger. Paulie wasn't visible through his windshield because of the bright lights overhead reflecting off the glass. Mike considered driving on but he couldn't, not and abandon Paulie. He had to do something.

Recognizing Paulie's mistake, Lee had pulled into line behind him, as if she could help by staying close. Now it all hit the fan. A cop had come from somewhere to join the argument. Cars behind them honked and one man got out of his car to shout something at the tollbooth attendant. To her left Lee saw a pair of darkened lanes, closed at this time of night. She acted without thinking. Without Mike here to tell her what to do next, without anyone's advice and counsel, she did something unthinkable only a week earlier. She took charge.

She cramped the steering wheel left, pulled the Honda out of line and darted through the nearer closed lane, her horn singing away into the darkness.

The trooper jumped to the step tread below Paulie's cab door and hung there in fear while he looked behind him.

"There!" Manny shouted. "That's your job! Go catch that car, if you . . . " He was talking to empty space, as the trooper sprinted for his idling patrol car, parked two lanes to their left.

"Mister?" Paulie tried again. He held out a fistful of cash, forty dollars, all he had in the truck with him. "If you just let me—"

"What are you waiting for, an engraved invitation? You think I got all night to waste on you idiots? Can't you see there's other people in line?"

Paulie dropped the bills fluttering to the ground and slammed the truck into gear.

Mike watched it all in his rearview mirrors. When he heard the Prelude's piping horn and saw Lee run the closed lane he understood her decoy tactics at once. He wanted to cheer. He blinked his lights and lumbered away from the curb with the big diesel engine roaring. The truck crawled, seemed to take forever getting underway, but he had enough speed to swing a big S-turn first left and then right to block the center exit lanes and shield Lee's car from the trooper's view. She had switched her lights off and drove in the glare of the carbon-arcs overhead. Behind them the trooper laid rubber and hit his siren, his red light flashing as he fishtailed away from the tollbooth and took up the chase; but Mike blocked his view for a few seconds, long enough for Lee to swerve right and bounce up over the curb and off the street onto a gravel lot holding two huge billboards—"Cherry Hill Mall," and "WISH-FM." The trooper added his horn to the screaming siren, then swerved left around Mike and roared away in pursuit of the wrong pair of taillights.

Lee had stopped and sat idling, lights off.

Mike slowed, watched the police car disappear into the night ahead of him.

Paulie had fallen in line again.

As the pair moved past her, Lee bounced back down into the street and switched on her lights.

The whole sequence took seconds and couldn't have come off better with hours of rehearsal. Mike and Lee shared a thought: to thank each other for their mutual quickness, but each stuck to the task of driving slowly, inconspicuously, down the half-empty streets.

The trio picked up speed as passing cars darted around the two in back to fill the intervals among them. In a few minutes all three—Mike in front, Paulie a block behind but moving closer, Lee far enough back to be one of several cars trailing along—had calmed enough to see where they were driving. And, unconcerned, the city of Camden swept past on each side.

Saturday night Lester-the-thief donned another of his many hats and became Lester Printz, dance hall proprietor and bon vivant. The relatives who cluttered his payroll all week picked up their salaries Saturday night and brought along friends to help them spend the money; former customers dropped in; Rolling Rock and Bud Lite flowed like water. Set-ups cost seventy-five cents. There was a knock-rummy game at a felt-covered table where the same six regulars had gathered Saturdays for eight years. More a family outing than a business operation, the weekly party was Lester's day of rest. Most busy Saturdays Camille and Lucille didn't get to bed before midnight, the first time, and they seldom got home to sleep before 5:00 AM. The gas station checkpoint out on the highway pumped gas on Saturday nights, as it did on summer holidays—for the sake of appearance—when the tourist traffic toward the ocean beaches was heaviest. Saturday night was special for Lester Printz. On that night, by choice, he didn't deal in hot cars.

For that reason he'd almost kissed off Paulie Klein's friend and his cockamamie notion of boosting a whole squadron of hot Cadillacs. The idea was crazy, impossible... and therefore worth testing. Because the only blot on Lester's record was a nagging inability to find enough Cadillacs to meet the market. Potential buyers from as far off as Florida and Texas dropped in to see him when they were in Philadelphia, phoned on Lester's toll-free WATS line, or queried his website (*www.lestercar.com*), and the answer he had to give them embarrassed him. He couldn't help them. So, if there was the slightest chance that the Bradley kid wasn't a complete flake, this Saturday night Lester Printz might bend a rule and become again, for a few very profitable minutes, Lester-the-thief.

Profit, he cared about. Within twenty-four hours he could unload nine Caddies without trying, simply by filling standing back-orders, and unload them at prices ranging upward from ten to fifteen thousand dollars. For that kind of money there weren't many things Lester wouldn't try.

Except dealing in hard drugs. That one scared him. It was the reason he resisted connecting with The Company. The Company asked its employees to handle all sorts of touchy merchandise. No one with a good head on his shoulders, whose snug fit he enjoyed, ever said no. Pete Aiello didn't like the word "No." Rather than risk getting handed a kilo of heroin to transport some night, Lester maintained cordial if distant relations with Aiello and The Company.

On this Saturday night he sensed strange currents in the air. He was about to change his usual pattern of operation, in itself a risky enough step. There was another problem, a small and possibly irrelevant fact that nagged at him like the beginnings of a toothache. Among the friends gathered to drink with the twins and dance to the Wurlitzer was a shiny-faced kid with green eyes, one of Aiello's number runners, Pig Valdosta. Lester disliked Valdosta for two reasons: Valdosta was, in however small a way, part of The Company and therefore an unwitting spy in Lester's bar; and Valdosta picked his nose. Some people distrust drunks, or loudmouths, or men with a cast in one eye. There's no logic in it, only emotion. Lester distrusted nose-pickers.

He sat behind his kidney-shaped desk, buttoning and unbuttoning his Venetian lace shirt, toying with the medallion that nestled against the matted hair of his chest. He watched Valdosta, who was unwilling to wait till the crowd thinned, making a fool of himself by trying to get Lucille off to her back room and onto her back. Lester didn't mind if the girls turned tricks in the two back rooms he let them use, ostensibly to rest and change clothes. Not paying them a salary, he could understand that they might want some spending money, along with the entertainment and flattering attention they got every night in his bar; but he didn't want an issue made of trips past him to those rooms, not with a crowd watching. He wondered if Valdosta was trying to trap him into some trouble with The Company. Aiello had all the girlie operations in the area sewed up tight and didn't like competitors. Tonight, especially, Lester didn't want Valdosta hanging around.

Forty-odd people packed the Quonset hut and shouted to be heard above the burbling din of the Wurlitzer, though the regulars knew the Rock Oldies in the machine won this same battle every Saturday night. George Zordich stood near the entrance, resplendent in the outfit he called his "Saturday night tuck." He had two "tucks" and alternated them on Saturdays. George was tall enough to see over the crowd. Most of the time his eyes remained fixed on Lester at the raised desk. He watched Lester wave greeting to latecomers or promise jobs to relatives returned from wherever it was they went when they were flush and didn't need Lester's help. Between them, George and Lester controlled the house. There were duplicate light switches at the door and beneath Lester's desk, phone linkups between the two men and the checkpoint on the highway out front. George's function these Saturday nights was to keep Lester from being surprised. No one entering passed him without at least a visual frisking, and no left unless Lester nodded from his command post toward the back of the hut.

Together they made a good team. With seldom a thought of his own, George understood, and often even sensed, what Lester was thinking. Lester's more sarcastic enemies reversed the equation and claimed that Lester thought like George. On this particular Saturday night the comment would have been less slanderous than true, for Lester had taken on one of his bodyguard's regular tasks: listening for the phone to buzz.

When it happened, just before midnight, he and George simultaneously picked up two phone receivers. Neither spoke. They both heard the watchman's voice say, "It's the goods, George. The kid just roared through here hell-bent for election. He's got twenty of 'em, like you said to watch for, and you ain't going to believe it when you see. Paulie Klein's with him, so scared you could crack walnuts between his knees."

They hung up their phones and Lester nodded. George ducked out the door to clear the parking area—no witnesses wanted—while Lester stepped down off the platform and made his graceful way through the packed house. He seemed to saunter, tossing greetings to each side, slowing to joke with someone as he passed, but in spite of working the crowd so he moved straight to the door. Only once did he stop, to whisper in Lucille's ear and nod, stone-faced, to Pig Valdosta. That should keep Pig busy for a while. No reason for The Company to know any of Lester's business.

Lucille shrugged and let Pig pull her past the large desk toward her back room. Lester continued, standing aside at the door to watch George herd in two surprised couples told to move their face-sucking from parked cars outside to the din inside the bar.

Outside, Lester nodded once more, and George locked the door. No one would interrupt them now.

All the way from Camden, Paulie had been crowding Mike in the truck ahead. Even now, jouncing along the rutted path through the pine woods, he clung so close that Mike kept tapping the brake pedal and trying to back him away to a safer distance with the flare of brake lights. Nose to tail, they thundered into the clearing, one hundred fifty feet of roaring, dust-roiling rubber and steel.

Here they were, as vivid as the picture in Mike Bradley's mind: cars and carriers worth a million, bearing down on this clearing in the woods, huge orange-and-green monsters with glistening grillwork mouths sliding to a dusty squat here in the darkness. Something Lester'd never even imagined pulling off. And he and Paulie and Lee had more than imagined it. They had done it!

"Holy Christ, Lester, look at that!" George waved at the loaded car carriers bearing down on them through the dust and looked for a place to hide.

Parked cars rimmed the clearing. Dust boiled up to settle over them as the trucks slid to a stop in the gravel lot. Before either of the truck cabs opened, Lester made his decision. He stepped into the glare of headlights and motioned for the lead car carrier to follow him. He guided it to the darkened hut on the left of the clearing, George slid open the end door and stepped aside to let the carriers enter.

It was cramped inside the Quonset hut but the trucks did fit, side by side. While Mike and Paulie met between the trucks for a hushed, hurried conference, Lester examined the merchandise. Six two-hundred watt bulbs dangling from wires overhead lighted the inside of the Quonset too well for him to doubt his eyes. There they were. New. All of them, twenty, loaded snug on the carriers, battened down, being delivered like so many cases of Bud.

"What do you think?" Mike said. He walked up, bright-eyed, high on the heady glow of success and primed for praise. In his expression Lester could see a new sense of confidence Mike hadn't worn at their other meeting only a week earlier, less cocky now but sure of himself in a quiet way. For the third time in as many minutes, Lester revised his estimate of Mike Bradley. And of the negotiations to come.

Paulie Klein shuffled his feet like a fighter psyched-up for the opening bell. His nerves showed, anticipation more than fear. Just then the girl walked in from outside.

Lester hadn't liked her on first sight. She was beautiful, and that meant conspicuous, and out of his league. The sardonic smirk she now wore did nothing to change his opinion. He'd prefer her not to be here; she made for an extra complication in dealing with Bradley.

Lester wanted . . . these . . . cars. Over a half million bucks retail stood right in front of him, their actual value to him dependent on his ability to haggle with these kids, and how fast he wanted to sell them: ten K apiece, overnight. Hold out for fifteen or more each, that would take a few days. But first he had to deal with amateurs he didn't know. Okay, they had pulled it off, somehow. Still, the horse-trading coming up was Lester's strength. He wouldn't be conned by them, no matter how smug they felt about their successful caper. There were different paths to consummation: ploys, feints, offers and counteroffers, a series of steps Lester had taken so many times that he knew the game very well. You don't get what you deserve; you get what you negotiate. Collect two hundred thousand dollars, do not go to jail.

Lester circled the loaded carriers again. Let the kids sweat a minute.

He took his time, examining the loads with half his attention while he tried to feel the mood Bradley and Klein had brought with them. Nothing wrong he could see. No bent frames. No retreads or bald tires gouged to simulate new ones. His practiced hand rubbed the smooth sidewalls of the tires testing for the checkering of age. Three cars at eye level on his left showed no oxidation in the chrome above the exhaust outlets. His probing finger gouged inside tailpipes and came out clean. No crusted oxides or accumulated oil scum. The cars were new.

How the hell'd you do it? Lester-the-thief wanted to ask them. But there was no profit in such a question. He maintained his poker face.

Mike Bradley was a card-player, too. "Satisfied?" he asked. He stood tapping a heavy envelope against his thigh with one restless hand.

"Maybe. You said there were papers?"

Mike handed over the envelope. "Twenty titles."

Lester took the envelope. Forge a few signatures, and there they were, ready to turn over to the next owners. It was too good to be true. He passed the envelope to George, who clambered atop the load to begin matching engine and frame numbers against the official papers.

"Okay," Lester said. "You did it."

"Can I tell you how?" Paulie danced forward, all eagerness. "You never saw anything easier, Lester. All we—"

"No, don't tell him," Mike interrupted. He shook his head at Paulie, smiling. "Does Macy tell Gimbels?"

"Are we competitors?" Lester asked.

"What's a Gimbel?" Paulie asked. "Oh, you mean that department store that went broke?"

"Not competitors. I'm just delivering these, as promised. One shot, and we retire from the business."

Lee walked closer to rest a hand on Mike's arm. "It's like we just won the gold medal," she said. "We don't have to prove anything else, do we, Mike?"

He squeezed her hand in delight at seeing Lester tilted off balance this way. He enjoyed Lee's understanding of the whole adventure. Maybe he'd propose again. He said, "That's it, Babe. Top gun doesn't go looking for fights."

George hopped down off the nearer load. "These check out, Lester. I'll look at the others."

"Skip it. Bradley here will get the idea I don't trust him." Lester smiled at the impatient trio. "Now, what do you say we talk money? Want to go inside? We'll have a beer, sit and—"

"Nothing to talk about," Mike said. "You need the cars, I brought them to you. On the phone we agreed three thousand apiece, and we can both handle the arithmetic. Twenty cars, three thousand each, an even sixty thousand."

Lester shook his head. "I was afraid this would happen. That'd be a fair price, if the cars were in the shape I need. But look here." He pointed at the nearer load. "There's not a white one in the bunch, and that means some repainting. You know what it costs me to repaint a Caddy? No, I think we've got to figure—"

"Sixty-one thousand," Mike said, in a practiced monotone.

"What?" Lester blinked at him, then felt his neck stiffen at Paulie Klein's' stifled laugh. "Look, kid, don't play your smartass games with me. If I say we'll talk, we—"

"Sixty-two."

"Who the hell do you think you are? How'd you like to turn around and take the whole bunch of them out of here? Maybe you can open a roadside stand, right? Put up a sign: 'Stolen Cars for Sale.'"

"Sixty-three thousand, and I'll throw in both the car carriers." Mike shook his head in warning. "Remember, Lester, I can take these out and drive them in the ocean, I don't need the money to live. I've got a job."

George watched the color flaring in Lester's neck again and stepped between the combatants to say, "Lester? We can use those trucks. I know you're the boss, but the price ain't that bad. If you want, I can make some phone calls and—"

"Shut up!" Lester snapped. Then, two deep breaths later, "Sorry, George."

"Okay." A sick smile moved his lips without reaching the rest of his face. "You're a ballsy kid, I'll give you that," he said to Mike. "Only I don't think I want to see you again.... George, pay him. I'll be inside." Lester pushed between Paulie and Lee, on his toes like a feisty bantam rooster, hoping for a moment that they wouldn't get out of his way.

They stepped aside to let him pass and then stood bracketing Mike to watch the cash being counted into his hand. Both were bursting to talk but a sense of ceremony in the air kept them hushed and deferential.

Mike studied George's face, not the bills piling soft in his palm. Without moving his eyes he handed Lee the money. "Carry this, Babe?" He waited, but George didn't offer to shake hands.

A sudden whoop from Paulie broke the mood. He took Lee's hand and pulled her running from the Quonset hut.

Mike strolled to the Honda, feeling George's eyes on his back the whole, slow, way.

Lester-the-thief stood in the shadows and watched the kids leave, his anger gone. It didn't matter to him who Bradley thought had got the better of the trade. Lester wasn't in business for the sake of his ego. After a painless five minutes of arguing, he had a building stocked with twenty cars he could turn into immediate cash. One hundred forty thousand or more profit is a good five minutes' work in any economy. If he had bought one car, or two, Lester would have left the

Quonset hut locked till Monday. For a score of them, he bent his rule about no-work Saturdays further out of shape and returned to the storage Quonset to watch George clean the cars.

On a workbench against the north wall, tossed atop a folded army blanket, lay the contents of twenty glove compartments. The cars were too new to offer much in the way of accumulated extra loot. Piled on the army blanket were three pairs of sunglasses, several maps, two Tootsie Rolls, a plastic rosary, Kleenex, a compact that might bring ten dollars from a jewelry store owner Lester knew in Ocean City, three combs, and a nutcracker but no nuts, lots of paper, miscellaneous junk, and of course no gloves. In seventeen years Lester had only once found a glove in a glove compartment. He poked through the junk, sorting out owners' manuals, service records, and warrantee books. It wouldn't do to leave the former owner's name anywhere in a car.

This first sweep in a thorough cleaning was George's job. He could be trusted not to keep any liquid assets he found. Others would later vacuum the interiors and trunks, checking for any identifiable scrap of paper or bit of incrimination hidden behind a seat cushion. Lester flipped through a service booklet: three-thousand-mile free checkup, by Colonial Cadillac. He snorted at the ornate endorsement embossed in the booklet. That was Aiello's style, all right, wasting money to impress people after the sale.

A second service booklet bore the same endorsement. Colonial Cadillac. This time Lester didn't find it amusing. He dug four more out of the piled junk. All the same. "George!" he shouted. He hadn't needed to shout.

George was standing beside him, hands full of license plate brackets. "Look at these." He handed one of the brackets to Lester and tossed the others to the bench. "They're all from the same place. Why do you think—"

"Leave them. I don't know what the game is, but I'm not playing. Let's go." He snapped off the overhead lights and led George into the parking lot. "Lock this place, then clear the bar."

"Clear it?"

"Out! All of them, and right now!"

George unlocked the front door of the bar and let a blast of noise escape when he pushed it open. One hand reached inside to flick off the lights. A moment of stunned silence later, voices inside built from a low, puzzled rumble to a panic-touched roar. People jostled one another through the narrow doorway and boiled out into the parking lot to shout questions no one could answer. Some carried sweating cans of Rolling Rock, others stumbled out struggling into whatever coats they'd been able to grab in the darkness, and all of them squinted as if looking for a clue. The din built and ebbed, people bewildered at finding themselves outside and silenced by the cool night air.

"First damn hand I had tonight. Whose idea—"

"Where's Ernie? Ernie, are you there?"

"Lester?"

"Who turned off the lights?"

"Anybody seen Lester?"

"Somebody get George, a fuse blew."

"Cops!" one voice shouted and helped scatter people milling near the door.

A car started, then another, headlights swept the gravel lot as drivers backed and filled, jockeying around to leave.

The first engine to start mobilized people unsure of what to do next. Everyone fled—most in a panic all the worse for their having no reason to run. Voices shouted names and begged rides out of this cul-de-sac. There were four grinding collisions in the parking lot. A Mustang and a rust-riddled Capri backed toward the open center of the parking area from opposite sides and met with a crash to lock rear bumpers and sit spinning their wheels in the roiling dust until they broke free and the Capri hurtled into the lot-side underbrush while the Mustang tried to climb a tree. Horns blared. People shouted. Two sobbing drunks stood patting the hood of the stalled Mustang as antifreeze from its shattered radiator sprayed their shoes a bilious green.

Lester ducked inside the darkened bar.

"Everybody out!" he shouted. "It's a raid! Get out of here!" He stepped aside to let several huddled, shadowy forms rush past him. Headlights outside completed what his shouted warnings hadn't and those few lying hidden in the bar lurched to their feet to escape.

In less than five minutes the bar was empty, the parking area emptying. Two minutes more saw the last pair of taillights disappear into the pines headed toward the highway.

The clearing was quiet. Dust hung in the air, and off through the trees lights flickered and lurched as cars jolted over the narrow path, escaping from unknown phantoms. Only the hiss of the Mustang's shattered radiator sounded in the sandy lot. George walked over to pick up the Capri's rust-pitted bumper lying bent in the midst of the clearing and dragged it off to one side.

Peace reigned.

George entered the bar and hit the light switch. "They're gone," he said.

The room was a disaster area, like every other Saturday night. Chairs lay overturned, drinks spilled, playing cards scattered on the felt-topped rummy table. Electric power restored, the Wurlitzer wheezed to life halfway through "The Hawaiian Wedding Song," and keening steel guitars climbed from bass to treble as the turntable built to normal speed. The whining music woke Camille from her pleasant stupor in one of the straight-backed chairs. Humming, she struggled to her feet to dance with no one. Lester cocked his head at George, who took Camille by the arm and guided her stumbling toward her room at the back of the hut. She could sleep it off there.

Lucille's door opened a crack. It swung wider to reveal Pig Valdosta, hair mussed and pants rolled under one arm, peering out. "Where'd everybody go to?" In his white jockey shorts and yellow ankle socks he looked like a crane.

"Get out," Lester told him. "Now."

"You're not the boss of me."

"No, but you might want to get to a doctor real fast."

Pig stood blinking. "Doctor? Do you mean Lucille is . . . ?"

"I mean in just about a minute George is going to walk over there and feed you one of your own arms up to the elbow."

Pig glanced from one to the other. Then, more bewildered by the empty, littered bar than frightened by Lester's threat, he scampered across the room. He stopped at the door to hop on one foot and tug at his pants. "But where—"

George planted a shoe against Pig's backside and helped him out into the parking lot. He slammed the door behind him.

Lester paced beside his desk. Twice he started to ask George a question but each time stopped himself. George didn't have any answers. "Okay, okay," he said. "Okay. I don't know whether they're stupid or they think I am, but okay. . . . George, you walk out and tell Jack to close the station. Then bring him back with you. We're going to have us a little meeting and get some things settled. And I got one call to make."

The door opened and Pig Valdosta peered in, one hand raised to ask a question. "One of you guys seen Ernie Rice? He give me a ride—"

"George!" Lester refused to look at Valdosta. "When I turn around that schmuck better be gone. You tell him that."

Pig was indignant. "Who you calling names, you fruit?"

"George!"

The door slammed, and Lester stood staring at his green princess phone.

Mike drove back into Philadelphia but took the long route south, crossed over the Walt Whitman Bridge, and headed north up Broad Street to Washington. No need for him to explain the detour. Both Paulie and Lee understood. The car might be recognized at the Ben Franklin tollgates, and the tollbooth attendant had spent too much time arguing with Paulie for them to be certain he wouldn't now see through Paulie's lack of disguise (his mustache was in his pocket). Mike drove with both hands high and white-knuckled on the leather-wrapped steering wheel, a steady 25 MPH.

"There's such a thing as too careful," Paulie protested. "Let your hair down a little. I mean, here we sit with better than sixty thou and you act like the new preacher in a small town! Can't we stop for a couple drinks, man? I'm wired!"

"At home," Mike said, and meant it.

Lee and Paulie grinned at each other when Mike swung a three-block detour to avoid passing the Colonial Cadillac showroom. They laughed aloud when he parked the Honda a long block away from Paulie's warehouse and asked Paulie to walk on ahead to open the door. He and Lee would follow some distance behind. They laughed, but they humored him.

Once inside Paulie's upstairs apartment, they stood watching. Mike held out one hand and took the money Lee gave him. He looked at it, at them, at the ceiling, stretching out the tension they all felt, and then with an explosive shout of joy he tossed the loose bills into the air. In a fluttering storm of green paper the three hugged one another and danced in a clumsy circle till they fell laughing and breathless to the floor.

"You did it, you really did it," Paulie wheezed. "Had me scared for a minute there, when that toll taker wouldn't—"

"You? How 'bout me?" Lee interrupted. "You think I wasn't having a bird when I drove through that closed tollgate? All the time I didn't know if they'd chase me or not."

"Or catch you," Mike said. He kissed Lee. "You pulled us all through, Babe. Trouble is, you're going to start liking the kicks too much. What happened to 'All I want is peace and quiet'?"

"Just try me!" Lee said.

And Paulie raised his hand in a silent vow.

Mike slapped the raised palm and said, "We did it, pulled it off, and no one hurt."

"And the people whose cars Lester has?" Lee asked.

Paulie smiled. "Insurance pays them all."

And Mike agreed. "Look at it this way. Paulie and I just drew an advance from our new employer." He took their hands to pull them into a close circle. "Home free, and more money than I ever counted on."

"Speaking of counting..." Paulie scrambled around on all fours gathering the scattered bills.

They sat at Paulie's table and worked out a split, not the fifty-fifty Mike had suggested in the beginning, and not the three-way division Paulie plumped for.

"Lee, Harry, and I, we're all one," Mike said. "We'll settle for sixty percent, you take forty. We couldn't have done this thing without you, Paulie, no kidding. Fair enough?"

"Fair? A quarter of the take's 'fair.' I didn't do squat, except almost screw you up. You were the one with the tough part. When I think of all the planning that—"

"While you two swap flattery, I'll phone out for some pizza," Lee said. "Time somebody got practical, and all this talk has got me starved." She motioned for Paulie's cell phone.

"You know I love you," Mike said softly.

"Not now," she warned him. "Pizza's as far as I go."

"Eating cheese? That's a concession."

"They'll make it cheeseless."

"'S'long as you're bending this far, you want to talk about a wedding?"

She caught the phone Paulie tossed her but before she could punch in the numbers, it rang under her touch. "Saved by the bell."

"Go ahead," Paulie said. "Let them think I've got an answering service."

He and Mike went back to parceling out the money. All fifties, crumpled and dog-eared, the bills made a pair of wonderful lopsided stacks, and both men enjoyed tamping the edges to straighten them. They couldn't stop grinning at each other.

"Klein Associates," Lee said into the phone. "Original designs by Paul Joseph Klein. This is Mister Klein's secretary."

Paulie whispered, "Tell them to paint the bedroom two coats and call me in the morning."

"Who? Well, I don't. . . . Uh-huh. I think. . . . " Lee debated, a frown creasing her forehead. "Mike. You better take it."

"Me?" He tossed the bills onto the table and bounced to his feet. Lee's next words took the spring out of his stride.

"Lester says the deal's off."

Exchanging a quick puzzled look with Paulie, Mike blustered with confidence he didn't feel. "Off, nothing! He's trying something to cut the price. Let me talk to him."

Lee joined Paulie at the table and watched. They sat frozen, trying to think of nothing, hoping for less. The old warehouse creaked around them, accentuating their silence. They heard only a dozen words. No matter what Mike started to say, Lester interrupted; and though Lester's words weren't audible across the room, his voice was—a tinny, shrill whine that marked an end to their short-lived celebration. When Mike said, "Soon as we can," Paulie shuffled the two uneven piles of bills together and rose, dusting his hands. "I don't think I want to hear this."

"There's a little problem," Mike began, after hanging up the receiver.

"How little?"

"Do you know someone named Pete Aiello?"

Lee shook her head. "Never heard of him."

"Everybody knows about Aiello," Paulie said. "Except nobody ever sees him anymore. They say he's The Company. But what's he got to do with—"

"This Pete Aiello, it turns out, or one of his people, owns Colonial Cadillac. Lester's scared and he gave us an hour to take those cars off his hands and return the money. Otherwise, he'll sic Aiello on us."

Paulie snatched up his sketchpad and was out the door before Lee could react.

She stopped Mike. "What does it mean?"

"It means we've got to put back all the cars."

"Take them back? But if Lester doesn't want them—"

"You're not listening, Babe. 'Take' them back is one thing. We've got to *put* them back, and before this Aiello finds out who took them in the first place."

She nodded, resigned, and once again became her father's daughter, her new-found confidence evaporated. "I knew it wouldn't work. We had everything going for us, all peace, and quiet, and now this. It comes from taking that dumb job. We just have to leave well enough alone."

"Don't, Lee, not now. We've got enough on our plate."

It was midnight, a new day.

"Let's do it," Mike said.

SUNDAY

"I'm getting to know this stretch of road, y'know?" Paulie's sick grin worked no better than his feeble joke.

Mike drove, Lee sat beside him glum and staring into the darkness ahead. Mike's silence had a translation: he was considering alternatives. After the emotional high of their success, he refused to share in the depression that settled over Lee. The plan wasn't at fault. Lester's panic didn't make sense. And Mike would point that out.

"Don't argue with him, okay?" Paulie said. "I mean, if he's right, if Pete Aiello and The Company really own Colonial, then we bought us some real trouble."

"Whatever."

"No, man, I mean it! Aiello'd just as soon see us dead as not, what I hear about him. And I don't feature swimming the Delaware in cement boots, you know? So what we'll do is, we'll get the cars from Lester and take them back."

"Just like that."

"Why not? It's dark. We've got all night. No sweat."

"And the money?"

That was the part that hurt. In his imagination, Paulie had already drafted the text of his invitations, in imagination had planned the entire ceremony he would hold in his warehouse. To come this close and then miss... "I know, but so what? Easy come, easy go."

Lee flinched at the word. "Easy? After everything Mike did? I don't like it anymore than you do, but let's see what Mike says we should—"

"I say we're not through yet," Mike told them. You trusted me this far. Don't let one little setback throw you. Wait and see what we can work out with Lester. Remember, he wants the cars as much as we don't want them."

Lester did... want... those... cars—but not at the price he could imagine having to pay. His independence was worth more, the right to operate here on the fringe of Company territory without interference. Even over a hundred-fifty thousand quick (and tax-free) dollars didn't compare to that. All he could think of was unloading these cars, fast, and without Aiello's knowing that Lester had ever seen them. Keeping his hands clean, that was Lester's immediate aim.

He paced the parking lot, waiting. George stood near the storage Quonset, Jack the watchman was in front of the darkened bar. Beside each stood a shotgun, butt in the dust. That was all the persuasion Lester would need.

Mike dimmed the Honda's lights to parking and got out. He assumed that Lee and Paulie would follow, though he wasn't certain, not after the Honda's headlights had shown them two men holding shotguns leveled on them as they approached. He tried to don a comfortable smile. After all, Lester and he were two businessmen, discussing a small misunderstanding. The shotguns were part of Lester's office furniture, like adding machines and filing cabinets. Nothing to worry about.

Lester held out his hand, palm up. "Let's have it."

"You're a great joker." Mike laughed. "What do you really want? If you think haggling price—"

"The money, kid, or I'll take it out of your bloody pocket after George blows you in half."

"He'll do it, Mike." Paulie stood beside him whispering and trying not to look as frightened as he felt. He clutched his sketchpad to his chest like a shield.

"Now wait." Mike stepped closer to Lester. "Look at it this way. You want the cars, and—"

"I don't want a thing but out of this."

"What does it matter to this Aiello character? Private citizens owned those cars. The fact that they bought them from Aiello in the first place doesn't mean they—"

"It means Monday morning Colonial Cadillac is going to look like a councilman's funeral. There'll be so damn many cops hanging around you couldn't count them all, and if there's one thing that makes The Company guys unhappy, it's lots of cops poking around their business. For any reason."

Again Mike tried to laugh it off. "All right, so this Aiello gets unhappy. But he doesn't lose anything by it."

Lester grabbed Paulie's arm and dragged him forward. "Tell your shit-heel friend, Paulie. If you're The Company and you get cops coming out your ass, what do you do about it?"

"Uh . . . well. Maybe I get a little sore."

"Yeah, 'a little sore,' and then maybe you look around for someone to lean on." Lester punctuated each phrase with a violent nod and shook Paulie by the arm. "And maybe you find all twenty of those cars sitting right across the river in Jersey, and then maybe you lose your temper and do something nasty, like you burn down these whole fucking woods!" He nodded, and nodded. "That's what maybe you do, am I right?"

Paulie was nodding now too. "Give him the money, Mike."

"You goddamn right, give me the money! And then you take those two carriers and you haul ass out of here!"

"But, where?" Mike asked.

"Where? Who cares where? Drive them into the ocean like you said, or take them back to Broad and Market and give them to the mayor. All I know is, they better not be within twenty miles of this place. You do that, you get them away from me, and I'll do you one big favor. I never heard your name, never saw the cars, nothing."

Lee stepped forward. "How do we know we can trust you?"

Lester stared at her a long moment. He still didn't like this pushy kid. "Okay. You know you can trust me because I say so, for one. And second, because what's it to me whether Aiello catches you? As long as he never tumbles that I knew about it, nothing. So no matter what, I don't mention your names. And then." His smile was ugly, all teeth but venom in his eyes. "Then, I know you won't mention my name, even if Aiello does catch you—which he's liable to do, by the way. I know you don't mention my name, because if that happens I get sore. And maybe I'm not as big as The Company, but I got a real good memory. Tell her, George."

"That's true." George waved his shotgun and moved Lee back two paces.

Stepping in front of her, Mike held out the stack of bills. "Here it is. Will you give us a couple minutes to talk?"

"I'll give you zip!" Lester said, taking the money. "I want you out of here ten minutes ago. The trucks are right where you left them. Get them moving."

Two shotgun muzzles urged Mike toward the storage Quonset hut.

"Lee? Follow us out. I'll stop somewhere on the way home."

They started the trucks. Backing out of the Quonset hut, Paulie tried to snag the doorframe with his wide load—it would work out some frustration to leave his mark on the place—but he missed and backed into the parking lot. Mike backed around him and led the way off into the pines. Before they left the clearing, Lester and his men had faded from sight.

It was after two in the morning when the trio drove through the empty barn, past the darkened gas station, onto the highway headed west toward Camden. The road was deserted. Bar lights had flickered off. Most motels wore "No Vacancy" signs, and small towns strung like beads along the highway were dark and silent. Although the meeting with Lester had confirmed Paulie's fears, Mike wasn't discouraged. Not with what he had noticed on his two trips out to Lester's from Philadelphia. He knew where they were headed, though discretion had kept him from naming a destination in Lester's presence. The deal wasn't off. It had simply changed in a few details, and as he wrestled with the truck's logy steering wheel he mulled over those details again.

Ten miles east of Camden he found what he was looking for. A turnoff to the left, flanked by two signs: "Millet Bros. Quarry," and "Trespassers Will Be Prosecuted."

Slowing to make certain the headlights behind him were close enough to mark his turn, he pulled off the highway onto a dirt road. In two hundred yards he stopped. A stretch of the road circling the top of an abandoned, water-filled quarry was wide enough here to afford turning space. Moonlight glinted off the water and turned the quarry into a romantic, secluded lake. He sat waiting for Paulie and Lee.

When their lights approached he took the milk crate that rested on the cab floor to his right, hopped down, and directed Paulie to pull up close behind his truck, Lee behind them both. That left room to turn the trucks around, though he had no intention of doing that tonight. Darkness and the screen of high underbrush concealed them from anyone passing by on the highway. He shivered in the chill air and waited for the others to cut their lights. Then he waved for Lee to join him, and both climbed into the warm cab of Paulie's truck. They sat on upended milk crates and looked at Paulie.

"Now what?" Paulie asked. "A meeting?"

"A little talk."

"Talk? We're going to run out of darkness. I mean, if we're going to spread these cars around where they belong—"

"We're not."

Sitting between the men in the truck cab, Lee slid her crate closer to Mike but leaned toward Paulie, by posture choosing both sides of the argument at once. "Maybe this once Paulie's right," she said. "It doesn't matter, Mike. We pulled it off. The rest's not your fault. If you say we give them back—"

"Lester said we give them back, not me. As far as he knows, right now we're scurrying around Philadelphia, doing that."

"But," Paulie said. "Isn't that next? You're going to say, 'but.'"

Mike nodded. "But why should we? When Lester took his money back, that paid him off. It's none of his business what we do with the load now. No one made him a partner."

Paulie reached behind his seat and dragged out his sketchpad. He balanced it on the large steering wheel, a comfort in plain view. "So what do we do? Leave the cars here?" His voice was plaintive with hope.

"We leave them here."

"That's more like it!" Paulie's relief filled the cab. "You had me scared there, man."

"Me too," Lee said smiling.

"We leave them right here, till tomorrow night."

"Oh, Jesus!" Paulie turned and stared out the driver's window.

"Now listen, both of you. What happens if we drive into Philadelphia tonight? Is anyone going to believe we're delivering these to a car dealer? This late on Saturday night? Half the agencies are closed tomorrow, and we'd be driving right into trouble, so—"

Lee laid a hand over his mouth. "You know what Paulie meant. Leave them! Saturday night, Sunday, what's the difference? Drive home and forget we ever saw them. Isn't that the safe way?"

Nodding enough to imply agreement, and to get Lee's hand off his mouth, Mike winked at her. "Sure, that's safe, if what we had in mind was walking away. But until we collect on those cars sitting back there behind us, we haven't finished what we started."

"Uh-huh. And how long till someone misses these car carriers?" Paulie asked.

"Couple days, anyway. Let's say Monday."

Paulie nodded in resignation. He continued to stare out his window. He knew nothing would change Mike's mind. He saved his energy.

Lee wouldn't be put off. "What are you talking about, 'collect'? If Lester won't take them, who do you think will?"

"Aiello."

It was very quiet in the truck cab. The windows had begun to mist over from their breath. The truck's heater fan still whirred though the engine was off. Mike waited a moment to give them a chance to digest the news. When it became obvious that they had either accepted it or were too stunned to protest, he said, "Aiello. If Lester's right—and you're both sure he is—the last thing Aiello wants is a big investigation of Colonial Cadillac. Okay, we'll help him. If he wants to keep his customers happy, and no cops around to pester him, he'll pay us to get these cars back. Let's call it a 'finder's fee.'"

Paulie said, "Mike?"

"It'll work, I know it will. If you want another name for it, what we did was store twenty cars, and we're taking care of them for their owners. If Aiello wants them back, and he does, he'll pay the storage charge."

Paulie said, "Mike, remember when—"

"Don't say anything about it now. I haven't steered you wrong yet, have I? Everything's worked like a clock.

We'll leave the trucks here overnight and go home in the Prelude. When I get things sorted out with Aiello, we'll pick up the trucks—"

Paulie interrupted again. "Mike, really, I've got to tell you—"

"What!" Mike slumped back and apologized. "Sorry, Paulie. Go ahead."

"You remember when we were in Colonial and I got shook because that cop came to the front door?"

"Sure, but—"

"And you remember at the tollbooth how nervous I got when that tollbooth guy wouldn't let me through?"

Mike laughed and reached an arm around Lee's shoulders to rumple Paulie's hair. "Everybody gets nervous sometimes."

"Yeah, but me, I only get that way when cops start poking around. And . . . now, I hate to say this, or you're going to think I'm a jinx, but Philadelphia, New Jersey, wherever we go, we've got cops coming out our ears."

"What?" Mike tried to sift through Paulie's hesitant comments. He and Lee caught on at the same instant. They twisted around to peer out the back window of the cab. Beyond the dark shapes of the cars loaded on the truck they sat in, they could see the glow of headlights. Lights ahead of them blazed and filled the cab with their glare. Headlights behind them, two pair in front of them.

"We're surrounded," Paulie whispered.

"Sweet Jesus! What is it?"

The headlights facing them dimmed, then moved past, as two cars unseen till that moment pulled out of the underbrush and drove along the dirt road back toward the highway. In passing they illuminated a sheriff's deputy in full uniform standing beside his patrol car with a flashlight in his hand.

Lee understood first. "We're in a lover's lane! The cops are chasing off kids parked here."

Her explanation didn't cheer them. The couples chased from their parking places had only to leave. They didn't have to explain a pair of loaded car carriers sitting in the middle of nowhere at 2:45 AM.

"Maybe he'll just go away," Paulie said. He slumped and pulled his cap lower. With one hand he wiped mist from the window beside him. "Then again, maybe he won't. Here he comes."

"Quick, Mike. Come here." Lee reached up to seize Mike's neck and pulled him into an embrace.

"What about me?" Paulie whispered in desperation.

A uniformed deputy sheriff aimed his flashlight into the cab. It waggled a few times, pointed up to throw shadows of Paulie's profile against the ceiling, and the deputy's muted voice grumbled outside the closed window.

Cranking the window down, Paulie said, "Ummm. You talking to me . . . to us?"

"What's it about, buddy?"

"I don't think I get you." Paulie stuck his head out the window while his right hand reached back across Lee and jerked at Mike's pants leg.

The deputy hooked a hand over the edge of the open window, stepped onto the tread atop the gas tank, and hoisted himself up to stand peering inside the cab.

In their embrace, Mike and Lee felt the cab tilt. They listened to a long silence. Bright lights shone pink through their closed eyelids.

The deputy swung his flashlight down and pointed it back at the patrol car as a summons. "Bert!" he yelled. "You want to come here a minute?" He tapped the flashlight on the door a few times before asking Paulie, "You think you could explain this so I could understand?"

"What's there to explain? You see. . . . Ummm. Would you happen to know the time?"

The cab tilted to the right as the deputy called Bert clambered up on the other side. He rapped on the window, forcing Mike and Lee to break their clinch. Trying to look surprised, Mike cranked down his window.

"Can I help you?" It sounded stupid, but nothing else came to him.

Now two flashlight beams played over the interior of the cab, swiveling and scanning like spotlights at a premier. Both deputies leaned toward the windshield and looked at each other past the trio sitting frozen between them.

"What did they say, Al?" Bert asked.

"We were just what you might call getting started," the first deputy explained. "But I thought I'd wait and let you hear it firsthand. You know, for corroboration."

"Is something wrong?" Mike asked, all puzzled innocence. He bit back a yelp of pain. Lee was squeezing his hand so hard that his knuckles ground together.

"I sure hope so," Al said. "Or unusual, anyway, else I been hassling the wrong kind of vehicles for years now."

"Ohhh, I get it. You mean the truck."

"Trucks," Bert reminded him. "Two of them. Two trucks."

"Can we let that go a minute?" Al asked. "I want to go back to before you walked up. I was asking them what was going on here. Now, from where I stand, it looked like the two on your side were playing suckie-face." He pointed his flashlight into Paulie's eyes. "Is that a fair description? They were making out?"

Eyes closed, Paulie nodded. "Yes. I think that's a fair description."

"I was hoping you'd say that. Good enough. They were making out . . . and just what the hell were you doing sitting here with them?"

"Me?" Paulie looked across at Mike, who was staring straight ahead, thinking. "Me? I was. . . . The heater in the other truck doesn't work."

"Right!" Lee chimed in. "It's warmer in here."

Bert shook his head. "Now you're confusing two kinds of answers. That's maybe why he was here, but it doesn't answer what he was doing here."

"Oh, *doing!*" Paulie nodded. "Yes, I see what you mean."

Al smiled. "What's so great about working with Bert, he goes to law school two afternoons a week. You won't slip any of your tricky diction past him." He poked Paulie with his flashlight. "Well?"

"Doing? You mean, what was I doing? Nothing, nothing special. I was just . . . Tell him, Mike."

"Sorry, Paulie, I didn't notice."

"Now that I believe," Bert said.

Paulie thought a moment longer, and gave up. "Drawing," he said. He held up his sketchpad for them to see. "I was drawing."

Al seemed to doubt him. "In the dark? You sat here in the dark while your two friends were . . . These two are friends of yours, aren't they?"

"Yes. We—"

"Good. No, don't give me any details. I want to take this one step at a time. While your friends here were doing . . . well, whatever they were doing, you were drawing."

"Here. Take a look." Paulie held out his sketchpad and flipped it open.

Al's flashlight played over it. Disappointed, the deputy said, "They're not dirty, are they? I was hoping for pornography. That way, I'd know what it is we're booking you for. As it is—"

"You mean arrest us?" Lee came to life. If Mike wouldn't talk them out of this bind, she would have to try. "I don't get it. All right, we were necking, but that's no reason to arrest anyone. If two people want to park somewhere, that's no—"

"You're not real precise, are you?" Bert shook his head. "Two people we see all the time, lotta times even fours. But it's you threesies that confuse us, if you follow me."

"Oh is that all." Mike smiled with ease. He was in gear again. He squeezed Lee's hand in thanks for her help and took over. "Now I see. You think the three of us . . . Uh-uh-uh," he shook his head. "Not a chance. These two are brother and sister, y'see?" He waved to indicate Paulie and Lee, black-haired Paulie and blonde Lee, sitting there trying to resemble each other. They failed. "He and I just got into town with these loads—we're taking them into Philly on Monday—and she came out to meet us."

"That's it," Lee said, snuggling closer to Mike. "We're engaged."

"Uh-huh, and then her brother got in the cab with us, because it's so cold in his truck."

The deputies squinted at each other, then at Mike. It was Bert who spoke. "Why'd he come along at all? Answer me that!"

"Good one, Bert," his partner said, and turned back to the trio. "He got you there."

Paulie was offended. "She's my little sister. Should I let her come out this time of night by herself?"

"If you think I'm going to believe . . . " Al dropped off the cab and walked in front of it. He beckoned to his partner. "Bert? You want to come here a minute?"

Through the misted windshield the trio inside the cab watched two silhouettes talking. Moonlight off the water-filled quarry shimmered around the pair of deputies, glinted off their silvered flashlights and badges. Before any of the three could formulate an idea worth discussing, Bert and Al returned—one at each cab window.

"I suppose you've got driver's licenses?"

All three reached for their wallets.

"No, no, no. I just asked if you got them, sort of because we're supposed to ask. I don't want to see them," Bert said. "Now, where are you headed if we let you go?"

"Home!" Mike snapped. "Uhh, their home! I'm just visiting."

"Yeah, I heard that one already," Al said, shaking his head. He didn't sound convinced. "I tell you what. Bert and I got rounds to make, and then we're off duty. After that, we're going to get in some pheasant shooting. Either of you two guys ever hunt pheasants?"

"Nope."

"Not me."

"Why ask them and not me?" Lee demanded.

"Do you hunt?"

"Of course not. Do I look like I'd murder a helpless bird?"

Al sighed heavily. "The point is, if we've got to fill out a lot of papers on you—all three of you—"

Lee nodded grudging thanks.

"—we'll be late getting started, and we want to be out on the ground at dawn, y'see?"

"Right," Bert said. "So if when we come by here on our way back to the station, we don't see anyone, well then..."

"We'll be gone," Mike promised.

"That's a real good idea." Bert and Al swept their flashlight beams around the inside of the cab once more. It was interesting to see. But only for a moment. "No drugs in there, am I right?"

"Drugs are poison." Lee was indignant.

"I just asked." Bert searched his mind and found it free of other troubling questions. "Okay then. We'll go make our rounds." He dropped from the cab-side tread.

Al jumped down and waited for Bert to circle the truck hood. "He was drawing, Bert, I saw it."

"I don't want to hear about it."

They walked toward their patrol car.

"Don't take my word for it. Go back and look."

"I don't want to go back and look. I said, drop it."

"Sure, Bert, only it's a fact. If he wasn't drawing in there, I'd say run them all in, and screw the pheasants."

"Don't tell me any more about him drawing."

"Sorry! Forget I said a thing! I won't mention it. Only he was drawing, and I didn't want you to think... Sorry, Bert."

After one last, weak attempt to make Mike see the wisdom of their fears, Paulie and Lee surrendered. Mike was adamant. He refused to abandon their prizes and instead sought a new hiding place. Once more the caravan set out, searching. In three separate vehicles but in one common state of shock, they drove back onto the highway, under reprieve.

There are problems involved in hiding two orange and green, seventy-five-foot articulated truck-and-semi-trailers, each carrying a quarter of a million dollars worth of spanking new Cadillacs. Only the belief that no one would be looking for the car carriers or the cars they carried till Monday kept Mike's battered confidence from collapsing. After two futile stops he found what he was looking for—what circumstances had driven him to—a truck stop motel with a vacancy.

The yawning night clerk gave them a room ($45 in advance) and showed them where to park the carriers, beside a furniture van from Charlottesville, Virginia, and a blue mobile home destined for Kutztown, Pennsylvania. He ignored their elaborate story about not wanting to drive into Philadelphia till Monday. After eight years of night work at the Hi-Way House Rest Stop he ignored everything truckers told him, counted them going into their rooms and counted the towels and ashtrays as they left. He waved them toward the farthest, dingiest brown cabin and went back to napping with his feet propped on an electric heater in his drafty office.

Mike and Paulie played out the charade. They entered the musty cabin and sat on a pair of twin beds as swaybacked as hammocks. After ten minutes to let the clerk doze off again, they ducked outside and walked a quarter mile down the highway, around a curve, to where Lee sat in the idling Honda.

It was nearing dawn. Their successful caper had so far cost them $114 in miscellaneous supplies and equipment, got them threatened with shotguns, nearly arrested (for the wrong reasons, though numerous right reasons for arrest existed); and the rising sun behind them didn't cheer them as it might have on any other crisp, cool morning.

"Sleep," Mike told them. "A few hours sleep and we'll be ready to go."

"Uh-huh." Paulie slumped in the backseat and thought of nothing.

Lee opened her mouth to argue. No squelch brilliant or telling enough came to mind, and she held that pose, sleeping, mouth agape.

Mike didn't mind the silence. He needed time to sift through ideas that kept blossoming fresh in his mind. Like a jazz musician, he let his imagination play riffs around a single theme. They were down; they weren't out. Although they hadn't yet converted to cash all those gleaming Cadillacs, Mike considered himself—compared to his net worth only twenty-four hours earlier—a wealthy man. He held that thought and took the long route south to the Walt Whitman Bridge. Where he borrowed three dollars from Paulie to pay their toll.

The clubhouse of the Trelawney Tennis Club (it's labeled TTC, on the ornate concrete crest above the entrance) sits perched atop a ridge overlooking Wissahickon Creek just outside Chestnut Hill. The clubhouse is four hundred years old. That's 397 years older than the Trelawney

Tennis Club itself. The clubhouse has occupied its present site for three years, transported stone by stone from Bury St. Edmunds, England, where it had served the Trelawney estate as a barn, until Theodore Winthrop bought and moved it. Four tennis clubs in Philadelphia had denied him membership—in collusion, he believed—and so he bought his own club. The Trelawney barn, disassembled, stones and beams labeled and shipped to America for reassembling, became the Trelawney Tennis Club, TTC. Although Theodore Winthrop's name appeared neither on the incorporation papers nor among the names listed as current directors, he owned and operated the club for his own pleasure.

It was his only public affectation. He didn't play tennis (because as Pietro Aiello he had never learned how), but he looked on the game as one worthy of his admiration and appropriate to his new station in life. Most of the club members knew nothing about Theodore Winthrop except that he reserved the center court every Sunday morning and never played on it. Instead, he sat in the clubhouse bar, before the huge plate glass window that filled in for a missing barn door, watching others play on the court reserved for his use and each Sunday released to the first member to ask him. Respectfully.

His tennis club had not brought him the happiness he had expected. He was happy. No one could argue that. But not because of Trelawney. Locating and buying the barn had been a game. Having it transported thousands of miles and reassembled was a challenge. But once the challenge was met, minor annoying disappointments began to accumulate. The stones of the building arrived in Philadelphia stripped of their four-hundred-year-old ivy, scraped and steamed clean by order of U.S. Customs and the Department of Agriculture. They might as well have been newly quarried. Then, for some reason, new ivy planted every spring and nourished through the heat of summer in a futile attempt to replace the old ivy died every fall. Bald spots showed on the walls like alopecia or the heartbreak of psoriasis. Two gardeners spent much of their time clipping and cleaning away dead foliage and replacing it with plants of a hardier strain. Those plants died as well. That was one disappointment.

Another involved the four tennis clubs whose refusal to accept Winthrop as a member had inspired his extravagant gesture in the first place. They ignored Trelawney and that galled Winthrop, who wanted their envy for the building and chagrin at having lost him as a member.

And yet a third disappointment: Winthrop discovered that tennis was a stupid way to spend a Sunday morning. Worse, maybe, even than golf. The players who grunted and wheezed through their rituals under his observing eye did the same things over and over. Arm back, pause, arm forward, pause. In between the arm movements there was too much running, shouted discussions about the stupidest set of numbers imaginable for keeping score, and more sweating than any man in his senses should be eager to buy. Particularly at forty dollars an hour.

In golf, Winthrop learned, if you screw up your first tee shot, you get a "mulligan." You get to do it over. Once. Screw up your serve in tennis (same as a tee-shot), you get to do it over, too. Not once a game (or "match," or "round," or whateverthehell), but every time! A mulligan, after every single serve! Dumb game.

Still, Theodore Winthrop wasn't a quitter. There had to be some reason why otherwise intelligent men enjoyed tennis, besides the chance to see one another in little white shorts. He hadn't discovered that reason yet.

Each Sunday he, Tiger, and Frank Guappo entered the Trelawney clubhouse bar at 9:30 AM. They sat at the center table, overlooking the center court, and drank Bloody Marys till noon, when Frank and Tiger were free to go to their homes, after they accompanied Winthrop to his. During that two and one half hour stretch Frank Guappo doodled on the white tablecloth, Tiger sat with his head swinging back and forth like a metronome timed to the thwack of racquets outside the window, and Winthrop listened to the conversations of other club members, all wealthy and for one reason or another denied membership in the same four clubs that spurned Theodore Winthrop.

On that late October Sunday morning, the three sat at their table. All wore tennis togs: white pants, white short-sleeved jerseys (why "white," Aiello/Winthrop didn't know. Actually, Winthrop didn't know, and Aiello didn't care.), and two of them had draped over their shoulders white cotton sweaters with the sleeves knotted in the front. Only Tiger wore his sweater. It covered "Death Before Dishonor" and a blue eagle tattooed on his forearm. (Winthrop doubted that tattoos belonged in the Trelawney Tennis Club; one tattooed applicant never learned why he'd been blackballed.) Tiger's Bloody Mary was untouched and would remain so all morning, because Tiger considered himself in training for his next fight. Frank drew squirrels and bunny rabbits on the tablecloth.

Winthrop drained his glass and reached out to set it on the table. It was a game he played almost subconsciously. Before the glass touched the table an anxious waiter hovering nearby slipped a silver tray under the descending, empty glass, and with his other hand placed a fresh drink on the table. Theodore Winthrop didn't like to wait, or even to ask, for service; and the help who worked Sunday mornings at TTC knew that. They knew that, or they didn't work many Sunday mornings at TTC.

The room was big, and it was cozy, those contradictions created by a skillful architect who had retained the low-beamed ceiling and stone walls but had mounted a walk-in fireplace opposite the plate glass window and had broken the wide expanse of stone end walls with ivy-filled planters. Voices carried well here, no matter how hushed the speaker tried to be. Through a fluke of acoustics, comments murmured in a distant corner bounced off the ceiling to settle on Theodore Winthrop's ear. By rotating his head left to right and back in a radar scan, turning to locate various speakers, Winthrop could eavesdrop on nearly everything being said, so long as the crowd didn't grow too loud or large enough to drown out one another. No fear of that on Sunday mornings.

The acoustics here had provided data leading to two hijackings, one short-sale of stock (Winthrop overheard a foundry magnate and his secretary at a secretive Sunday brunch, planning to elope with company funds), and several discreet touches of blackmail. Tennis was a stupid game. But Theodore Winthrop got something out of his Sunday mornings at his special table.

What he got this Sunday morning was a growing sense of unease, capped finally by recognition of a problem.

Outside in the crisp fall air a new tennis ball was beaten back and forth, trading its original fuzz for a slick orange tinge from the clay courts. Two men in their thirties had some sort of grudge match going, from the look of high color each wore and the determination they showed in violently slamming the ball to the ground between their powder-puff serves. Inside, in the cozy warmth of the bar, beginning to work on his fresh Bloody Mary, Theodore Winthrop picked up an interesting conversation.

Two men were complaining about their cars. Not in itself unusual, but one of them kept hammering the word "Cadillac." His had been recalled on Saturday for brake repairs, some factory oversight to be corrected. That interested Winthrop. He owned a new Cadillac stretch-limo and knew of no problems with it.

"Frank? The new car been giving us trouble?"

"How's that, Mister Winthrop?"

"The brakes. Do they seem bad to you?"

Frank thought a moment. Then, because he was being distracted, he reached over to grab his brother's neck and stop Tiger's head from ticking back and forth, at least till the pair outside finished their argument and resumed hitting the orange ball. "To tell the truth, Mister Winthrop, I don't believe as how they do. Any reason you ask?"

"Skip it, Frank."

Winthrop twisted slightly in his chair to find better listening post. He glanced around the dim room and located the men speaking at a corner table. One of them continued his tirade about shoddy Detroit workmanship and the threat of creeping socialism. A third man, Fred Enright, joined the pair and after perfunctory greetings began his own lecture.

"Know why I'm late?" Enright asked. "I'll tell you why I'm late. It's not bad enough getting home a day late—snowbound in Denver, would you believe that?

But then I walked into the middle of some dinner party Lois never bothered to tell me about, and found out she'd sent the car in to have the brakes fixed. This morning she and Jerry Long were meeting some people at the Marriott, I don't know what it was about, and I had to drop them there on my way over. One week I had that car, and *pffft*! Back she goes. A new Cadillac—"

"—same thing happened to mine last—"

"—and what happened? I always say you can't—"

"—week. Running along like a dream, and then Saturday I get this—"

"—trust a jock. King Kolchak may be a nice guy, but what he knows about cars you could pound up your—"

"—phone call. Colonial Cadillac is sending a man out to pick up my—"

"—up your—"

"Frank? Will you stop drawing on the tablecloth while I'm talking to you?"

"Sorry, Mister Winthrop."

"I'm getting a bad feeling about this."

"You want me to get you a doctor?"

"Get my phone out of the car. Right now."

Frank Guappo dropped both hands to the arms of the captain's chair to hoist himself erect when the waiter assigned to Winthrop's table appeared carrying a cell phone. He laid it in front of Winthrop and backed away, bowing.

"Good boy." Winthrop winked at the waiter and leaned closer to Frank, waving one thumb in the waiter's direction. "Find out that boy's name, and get King Kolchak on the phone. Tell him to meet us at the agency." He kicked his chair back—the waiter caught it before it tipped to the floor—and Winthrop tapped Tiger on the shoulder. "The car, Tiger."

Frank made the call. Theodore Winthrop went to take his post-tennis shower, and Tiger Guappo walked out to get Winthrop's stretch-Cadillac from its reserved parking spot. His head was still swiveling back and forth. The time was 11:35 and Tiger had twenty-five minutes more of Sunday morning tennis watching wound into his biological clock.

King Kolchak took an hour to shave, breakfast, and drive to the facility he called his car store. When he arrived Theodore Winthrop's limousine was already parked in the alley behind the agency. Kolchak didn't notice it. He was irritated at having his Sunday interrupted and noticed very little of what was going on around him. He fumbled with the back door key for several minutes, managing to lock the unlocked door and then try all the keys on his key ring one by one till he returned to the right key and reunlocked the formerly unlocked door he had locked.

Inside, Winthrop sat on one of the velvet couches in the rear corner of the showroom. Tiger and Frank stood beside the couch. Their presence surprised and confused King. Something about them didn't look right. And he hadn't known they had a key to his car store.

"Mister Winthrop, this is Sunday, and I don't have to—"

"Shut up, King?" Winthrop asked.

"Now listen. On Sunday I never—"

"Shut up, King." Winthrop suggested.

"And don't tell me to shut—"

"Shut up, King!" Winthrop ordered.

Kolchak clenched his fists and looked around for something to hit. "You've got a lot of nerve, coming in—"

"Shut up, King," Frank Guappo recommended. His fists weren't clenched, but they could get that way.

King looked from one to the other in frustration, then exercised that frustration by snapping at Tiger, the only one who hadn't so far attacked him. "You! Have you got something to say?"

Tiger started to shake his head. His brother reached out to seize his neck and stop him. No sense letting that get started again.

"King, sit down and listen. And think! How many new cars have you recalled for modification?"

Kolchak heard the urgent tone in Winthrop's words without understanding their meaning. He sank to the couch beside his number-one fan and sat wary. He sensed trouble in the air. Beyond that, this whole meeting was a mystery to him.

Winthrop patted Kolchak's knee. "All right, King. Let me put it another way. Some of the cars you sell have minor mechanical flaws . . . things wrong with them. Say the backup lights don't work, or a door handle sticks, and you have to tell the owner you'll fix it free. Do you understand that?"

Kolchak nodded, still wary . . . till the light came on. He knew what was throwing him off! Winthrop's two assistants were wearing white, like doctors, rather than wide ties. That's why their appearance troubled him. It must have something to do with Sunday. That detail settled, King could relax. He nodded again.

"Fine." Winthrop patted his knee again. "Now, have you done much of that?"

"Not that I can think of."

"Saturday did you call in two cars to fix their brakes?"

King relaxed even more. Whatever the trouble was, it didn't involve him. He smiled. As an afterthought, he reached over and patted Winthrop's knee. "It couldn't have been us, Mister Winthrop. The service department is closed Saturday, except to finish up work left over from Friday. We don't start any new stuff till Mondays."

Winthrop considered that fact for a moment. "Fine, King, that's fine. Now, I want you to go into your office with me and make some calls. You're going to phone everyone who bought a new car from you in the past month, and—"

"Why should I?" Kolchak started to rise, in his mind visions of missing all afternoon in front of the television set, both ends of the NFL doubleheader, unless he could turn on his office TV set.

Frank Guappo's hand pushed him back to the couch. "You'll do that because Mister Winthrop says you'll do it."

"That's a good point," Winthrop agreed, "but also you'll do it because you're interested in finding out who's satisfied with their car and who's not, and who thinks there's a brake problem, and so on. You're going to do a very subtle.... Sorry. A 'careful' way. You're going to find out whether anyone thinks you recalled his car. I'm getting a bad feeling about all this." He stood and led Kolchak into his office, to the files and a phone. Then he sat coaching Kolchak on his dialogue.

An hour later he had learned enough. Seven new cars were missing, perhaps more, and the break-in less than a week before began to appear part of a pattern. He had too few pieces in hand to understand the entire picture, but he would work at it. He talked over his ideas with Tiger and King, who listened, and with Frank, who listened and understood. In a few minutes he had worked out a set of assumptions; proven, they would lead to a plan of action that so far remained only the vaguest germ in his imagination. He asked Frank's opinion.

"It's not anybody from New York, unless they're looking to start up the troubles again, like before."

"Agreed, Frank, not New York."

"I don't believe as how it was nobody we know, if you want the truth. I mean, that would be real stupid."

"Agreed."

"And that means it's somebody on their own. Nobody we pay's going to fool with none of your property."

"You're still right, Frank. Now tell me this. Who's the only pro around who's not in with us? That little fag over in the Jersey, what's his name?"

"Lester. Lester-the-thief. Only I ain't sure he's a fag, Mister Winthrop. He only wears them fruity clothes."

"Uh-huh. And he hangs around with some blond guy named George."

"George Zordich, his name is, only I don't think he's no fag either, Mr. Winthrop. And even if he is, I ain't so sure about Lester."

"That's as may be. But if you swim with a duck, and you have feathers like a duck, and you're yellow like a duck, and you quack like a duck... well then, Frank, you're a duck. Lester-the-thief is a duck."

"If you say so, Mister Winthrop," Frank agreed out of habit. "He's pro'lly a duck, only I don't think he's no fag."

King Kolchak listened uncomprehending to this conversation about ducks and fags. It didn't mean anything to him except that he and Theodore Winthrop had finished their business. "Well, I'll be getting on home now—"

"Sit down, King." Winthrop paced in Kolchak's office. He straightened a few items on top of King's desk, shined a shoe on the back of his trouser leg, fidgeted about and let his body do what it would while his mind raced. "You're going to sit right here till we get to the bottom of this. And until—"

"Bottom of what, Mister Winthrop?"

Winthrop counted to ten, reminded himself that he couldn't put someone with Frank Guappo's arrest record in charge of Colonial Cadillac, located the strength for a faint smile, and said, "Tell him, Frank."

"Kolchak. Somebody's stealing your damn cars."

"What?" King leapt to his feet and looked out the office window.

"No, King." Winthrop motioned for him to sit again. "Not now. Yesterday, someone stole several of your cars. That's why those people you talked to on the phone thought you had their cars here. No, no, wait." He waved off Kolchak's protests. "I know you don't have them, but somebody does. And my guess is it's the same somebody who broke in here last Monday night."

King reached into his top desk drawer and took out the Xerox picture of Paulie Klein's privates. "This one?" He looked at it, discovered he was holding it upside down, and rotated the crisp sheet of the paper. "I mean, this one?"

"Right." Frank Guappo grew helpful. "What the cops call a male Caucasian of a unspecified age. Besides also he's a Jew."

Kolchak peered at the photo. "A what?"

"He's been snipped," Frank said.

"Put that thing away," Winthrop ordered. "Anymore everybody gets snipped. . . . Now you get me some answers. Frank, you ask a couple boys to help you. Ask around. See what they know about this Lester and his operation. Maybe Ernie Rice or Pig Valdosta. They live over in Jersey."

"Yes sir, Mister Winthrop."

"King, you and I and Tiger are going to sit right here in case any news develops. You know where to phone me, Frank."

Frank nodded and left.

"Can I at least turn my TV on?"

"Be my guest." Winthrop walked out of the office and back to the comfortable velvet couch to read a magazine. Tiger followed him, because Tiger always followed him. And Kolchak turned on the office television set to begin his Sunday afternoon vigil. The time was 1:04 EDST, and *The NFL Today* had just begun.

"I still don't think there was anything wrong with the plan, except overconfidence. I went into it without enough information." Mike tapped a pencil point on Paulie's worktable as he talked, trying to confess failure without sounding pessimistic. He knew that they could recover from this little setback. All he needed was to bring Paulie and Lee to the same state of confidence. "This is a joint stock company, not a dictatorship. We're all partners. I was wrong not to ask your help, but I'm asking you now. All three of you. Can we do this together?" He stopped, and waited.

Lee and Paulie nodded with little hesitation and leaned across the table toward him. Harry hadn't heard what was said. He sat on Paulie's couch, plugged into the transistor radio he wore, his hands plucking at the lap robe that swaddled his legs. He had come to Paulie's apartment under protest and now concentrated on a running argument about police department horses in Fairmount Park, the burning issue that occupied *The People Speak Out* this Sunday afternoon.

The three in Paulie's apartment—excepting always Harry, a silent fourth—agreed. All unanimously, though each independently, had reached the same conclusion. They would go ahead.

Paulie's decision had been easiest to reach: he had decided not to worry about it all and would go along with whatever Mike said. "A dictatorship's fine with me."

Lee's decision might be summarized in the same terms, except for one major difference, the route by which she reached it. Somewhere underlying all of Mike's recent moves there was a secondary plan that involved her. It was probably their marriage, which she opposed and would welcome. She wasn't clear on the details but knew that nothing Mike had done in the eight months they had lived together was selfish. He thought and planned for both of them. He'd put it in his own words to Paulie when they'd discussed splitting the take: "Lee, Harry, and I, we're all one." There it was—the reason she loved him. His ambitions always included her; yet throughout the past week she had found herself dragging her feet. Her fear of change took on new focus: she could face any sort of change, any new state of affairs, except one without Mike. Lee came to Paulie's conclusion, with one important difference. Whatever Mike wanted, Paulie would agree to. Whatever Mike wanted, Lee wanted as much, or more, for all of them.

As for Harry, he neither understood nor cared about the whole confusing business. For a man in his state of health, he told them, it was not smart to buy a green banana. He accepted his meager portion of life's travails one depressing day at a time. Harry ignored Mike's apologetic comments.

Lee said, "No, it's my fault. I haven't been helping the way I should, but I'll be better, wait and see."

And Paulie said, "Let's go for it."

"That's the problem," Mike said. "To get in touch with Aiello, without him getting a grip on us."

Shrugging, Paulie said, "I know a couple guys who run numbers for him, but they won't stick their necks out talking to a stranger, and if I talk to them . . . *whoooosh!* There we are, gigged. Besides, they're so far down the pole they probably never see a big guy like Aiello."

"Horseshit on the grass," Harry said.

His comment wasn't a contribution to their planning, only a reply to the conversation droning through his earplug.

Three times Mike talked them over a series of hurdles, different routes to the same finish line. Any of the routes might work, all of them might, but none was in the least useful because of a common fact. They all ended at a brick wall. "We've got to get to Aiello."

A voice said, "You won't like it when you do."

Lester-the-thief stood in the doorway.

"That big door downstairs is open, Paulie. If it was me The Company was out hunting, I'd put in some good locks." Lester stood peering over his sunglasses, waiting posed, as if on display. From the soles of his brown Wellingtons and the bottom of the orange bellbottoms he wore, to his tan turtleneck sweater and the gold beret on his head, he was a palate of fall colors, Harlequin gone autumn. "It took me two calls to find out where you live. How long do you think it will take Aiello?"

"Yeah, but you knew who you were looking for," Paulie said.

"So will he, soon enough."

"Maybe not," Mike said.

"Do I stand here all day, or do you let me sit down?"

"Come in, I guess," Paulie said. "Only we don't want any trouble."

"When you screw with The Company, you got to expect nothing but trouble." Lester entered and took the empty chair at the table while Mike, Paulie, and Lee sat waiting. He glanced at Harry for an instant. From the look of him, Harry didn't matter. "Let me guess you didn't start out on purpose to jerk Aiello's chain."

Mike nodded. "Absolutely! We didn't know—"

"Your dumbass play got me caught in the crunch, you know that?"

"We didn't ask you to come here," Lee told him.

Lester cocked his head her way. "Now, why is it you and I don't hit it off, Honey? Why do you suppose that is? The first time I saw you I decided I could get along real good if I never saw you again."

Lee slid her chair farther away from him. "Right, Honey."

"You didn't come here to tell us that," Mike interrupted. "What's going on?

"The last thing I need is Aiello on my back. And now, on account of you, that's what I got. He says—"

"You mean he knows?" Paulie stood, whispering.

"He knows zip. Now sit down, before I'm sorry I came. He don't know shit about you and me. All the same, one of his spooks comes over to my place an hour ago, throwing his weight around, asking did I know anything about two truckloads of new Caddies floating around Jersey somewhere."

"Then he does know." Paulie looked around for his sketchpad.

Mike waved him quiet. "No he doesn't, or Lester wouldn't be here right now."

"You got it, kid. He owns a couple guys who work on the bridge. Nothing much gets in or out of Philly without them seeing it, and they gave him a story about two loaded car carriers going through Saturday night. So all he knows is, you got to Jersey with his goods. And this creep of his, a punk named Valdosta, he comes by my place and says if I know what's good for me I won't have a thing to do with it, except maybe I should talk to Aiello if I hear anything."

"What did you tell them?" Mike asked.

Lester leaned back in his chair and let all three of them stare their urgency at him. It was his show. He shook his head in mock sadness.

"And I suppose the taxpayers buy the hay," Harry blurted.

Lester looked at Harry and leaned closer to ask, "Who does that one belong to? Paulie, you're getting yourself in bad company, you know that?"

"He's my father," Lee said.

"Why does that not surprise me?"

"Please!" Mike got their attention. "What did you tell this Valdosta?"

"I told him *nada.* Not fact one. Why should I? Aiello's got the manpower, let his army dig it out. Only the point is, they will. He'll poke and nose around, and then the first thing you know he'll hear something, and then something else, and then he'll put the pieces together. He's one smart son of a bitch. So I'm here to give you some good advice. Give the cars back."

"Oh, man!" Paulie nodded till his neck ached. "That's the truth. Only how?"

"I'm coming to that." Lester counted on his fingers. "One, I'm happier if he doesn't know I ever heard of you kids. So think what I risked coming here, okay?"

The three nodded. And listened.

"Right. So two, Valdosta tells me he's spreading the word. If whoever's got the cars shows their face anywhere, somebody will let them know to take the cars back to the Colonial lot down Broad. Take them back, leave them sitting out front there, and it's all over. Clean, and no trouble, no questions asked."

Smiling, Paulie subsided. "Thanks, Lester. Thanks a lot. Now all we—"

"Do you believe that?" Mike asked.

Lester shrugged. "Maybe. Only maybe also Aiello decides to make an example out of you. You know, kind of to discourage other people from messing with his goods."

"Uh-huh." Mike nodded and saw the same understanding in Lee's eyes. "It's a trap."

"Who can tell? I know this. If you can unload the cars and there's no way for Aiello to know you ever had them, then that's the smart thing to do. Only I kind of hope you rape the bastard."

"You do?" Paulie was curious. "Why?"

"Who the hell does he think he's talking to, sending Pig Valdosta out to my house? He can at least come himself or send one of the Guappos. And more yet, just because he can't keep track of his own goods, why should I save his ass?" Lester pushed back from the table and stood to give them a parting word. "So if you burn him good, I won't cry one little tear, you understand? Now, I only heard a piece of what you were saying there before I walked in. Not all of it."

Lee glared her doubt.

"No, no, no kidding. Not all, just the tail end. And maybe you can do it. Only let me give you a tip. Aiello says bring back his cars and it's all over. Except, while I'm driving in to come here, what do you think I see sitting by the bridge ramp there at Fifth and Locust? Two cars full of Aiello's soldiers, and they're watching the bridge. Want to bet there's more of them at both the other bridges?"

Mike rose to shake hands. "Thanks, Lester. We appreciate all you—"

"Don't appreciate anything. I'm still not happy you tried dumping The Company's cars in my lap, dumbass mistake or not. But also I'm not happy about punks like Valdosta who go around cock-of-the-walk calling people names. That stupid nose-picker insulted me in front of my kids! My wife and I teach them to respect their elders, and he—"

"Your kids, you said? You're married?" Lee was stunned.

Hands on his hips, Lester stared at her. "What now, am I supposed to show you a wallet full of pictures? Sure I'm married, why the hell else you think I'm in this business? You try feeding six kids today on a one-man salary."

"He's got six kids," Lee said to no one, trying to comprehend.

"And George to take care of, and Lucille and Camille. You think I don't worry about them? Same way Bradley here takes care of you people."

Paulie smiled as if he'd just been proven right in an argument no one had expressed.

Lester shook his head and turned to Mike. "Aiello's at the Colonial showroom all day, waiting to hear something. That's where you get in touch with him. Only remember, if you slip and he catches you, I never heard your name before. You mention me once, no matter what he does to you, I do it ten times worse."

"You ever smell a sweaty horse?" Harry asked, with a sardonic laugh.

Lester glanced from Lee to Harry and back. "It's an old saying, 'The apple doesn't fall far from the tree.'" He pointed a finger at Paulie. "Strange people," he said, and left.

Mike reached for the phone, but Harry already had it in his hands.

"Harry? Can you let that go? I've got to use it."

"A man can only take so much. I'm going to tell them—"

Mike cut off Harry's call. "Later. This is important, Harry."

"Important, huh?" Harry looked to Lee for support. "Just once, I'm going to tell off those idiots. Now they're talking about mounted police down in the subways!"

"Skip it, Daddy. Write it down like you always do. Let Mike have the phone."

Harry was offended. "Always Mike, isn't it? What about me? I never called in yet, but there comes a time—"

"No speeches, Daddy." Lee took his arm and led him to a chair. "You can call the radio station later. Mike's arranging it for you."

"Mike is? I can make my own calls. What does he know?"

"I know this better work."

When the phone rang King Kolchak sighed and turned down the volume on his TV set before answering it. "Colonial Cadillac. This is King Kolchak.... Who?...No, I think you've got the wrong number."

"Who is it?" Winthrop stood in the doorway with an opened copy of *National Geographic* dangling from one hand.

"Wait a minute." Kolchak covered the mouthpiece with his hand and said, "It's a wrong number, Mister Winthrop. They want to talk to somebody named 'Peter Yellow.' I told them—"

"Get the number and say Aiello will call right back....Don't argue. Do it!"

King shrugged and said, "Hello? If you'll give me your phone number he'll call you back....What do you mean, you won't give me your number? Why not?"

"I'll take it." Winthrop snatched the receiver from King's hand and motioned him back to his chair. "Who's speaking?...That's my name, who are you?" Winthrop pantomimed writing and got Kolchak to hand him a pencil. "Before you go through all this, let me give you some advice. I don't think you realize who you're dealing with. If you're smart...All right, go ahead." He scribbled notes on the cover of *National Geographic,* the magazine braced against the wall with his left elbow and the phone propped on his shoulder. "I've got it. Now.... 'Read it back!?' I don't know who the hell you are, but you're begging for a real load of trouble. When I.... Hello?" He slammed the phone down. "The son of a bitch hung up on me! On *me!*"

"Trouble, Mister Winthrop?" King asked.

"I'll nail his hide to the wall! Wait till I—"

"Who's 'Peter Yellow'? And what kind of name is that? I don't think you ought to take somebody else's phone calls. What if this Yellow—"

"King, get out of here. Go home. That's all, just go home, and don't come back till tomorrow, understand?"

Smiling, King said, "Now you're talking. And don't worry, Mister Winthrop. I'll find out about those stolen cars. But it doesn't matter, you know. The cops and our insurance company can work it out."

"Insurance company?"

"Sure," Kolchak said. "It won't cost us anything. Insurance pays it all."

Winthrop stared at him a moment. "King, do you know the name of the company you're insured by?"

"Yes sir!" he said, proud of his memory. "Hurtage Old-Time Fiddle-dee."

"Right, King. Go home." Winthrop motioned for Tiger to stop blocking the doorway and let Kolchak leave. He waited a moment before the phone rang again. "Yes?" he said. "Speaking. Go ahead." He read from the magazine cover. "Thirty thousand in used bills, none bigger than a fifty. Meet at entrance to Pier Thirty at ten tonight.... What makes you think I can raise that kind of money on Sunday?... Then you *do* know who you're talking to! All right, the smartest thing you . . . " His voice dropped to an awed whisper. "The son of a bitch hung up again!"

Winthrop paused only an instant before his sweeping hand jerked the phone out of the wall. He stalked from Kolchak's office and, passing through the doorway, paused to punch Tiger Guappo in the gut as hard as he could. Tiger blinked twice and stared down at his belt buckle, but by then Winthrop was halfway out the back door, shouting, "Move it, Tiger!"

They were back in action. Daunted. Threatened. Uncertain. And determined. Mike tried his best "command voice," fooling the other two if not himself. "Harry will run you both across the river to the motel. When you get my call, you hustle back. Got it?"

Lee and Paulie nodded, both reluctant to talk for fear of letting nervousness sound in their voices. Lee wore a jacket over one of Paulie's old shirts and a floppy pair of glue-stained khaki pants. Her hair was tucked up under a baseball cap, face scrubbed shiny, and Mike's auburn mustache stuck in place. At a quick glance, her beauty was hidden under the slight disguise.

"You sure you can handle that truck?" Paulie asked her.

"If I can," Mike said, "she can. Right, Babe?"

"As long as Paulie doesn't play any games at the tollbooth. I'm fresh out of ideas."

"Don't even joke about that!"

Mike hugged them both, and the pair of truck drivers shook hands. "Harry? I need you back here as fast as you can make it. Don't let me down, now. Sixth and Vine, in the park across from the police Roundhouse."

"Yeah, yeah, yeah." Harry tightened his muffler. "Chase here, chase there, while you sit around being the mastermind."

"I'll be busy enough. I've got to phone a messenger service. Take it easy," Mike said.

He gave them ten minutes lead time before he left the apartment, time enough for him to sit and try thinking like Pietro Aiello. It was a chess match, a contest. Aiello's carloads of goons waiting at the bridge were part of a predictable defense, the pair of phone calls an attack. Tonight would see them approaching the end game, and Mike wanted to consider possibilities. He didn't know his opponent well enough to feel comfortable. He decided to attack the reputation people described, rather than the personality no one seemed to know.

When he trotted down the rickety stairs to the warehouse below, he carried, wrapped in a brown paper bag, a table knife from Paulie's kitchen drawer.

At a People's Drugstore on South Street he bought an eyebrow pencil and a pair of nylon pantyhose.

He was ready.

Pier 30 sits at the foot of Kenilworth, a narrow, badly-lit stub of a street a short two blocks long, rising from the river to cross Front Street and dead-end at Second. On one side of the street is a muddy empty lot that will someday be filled with authentic imitations of eighteenth-century row houses, when all the existing shells in Society Hill have been expensively restored to their inexpensive original condition, and when the insatiable yuppie demand for "cramped-but-quaint" calls for more old-looking new construction. On the other side of the street stands a pair of empty warehouses in no better repair than the one Paulie Klein lived in. And on Second Street there are nondescript three-story buildings, a few inhabited, most boarded up. Of all the streets ranging north from Washington to Pine, where new landfill breaks the comb-tooth effect of piers jutting out into the Delaware River, Kenilworth affords the best view of the piers, and the only safely distant view of Pier 30.

Theodore Winthrop sat in the backseat of his stretch-Cadillac parked outside an empty warehouse between Front and Second on Kenilworth to watch a scene unfold before him, a scene safely distant from his vantage point but under his direction. Frank and Tiger were in the front seat of the car, slouched low for two reasons: Frank's reason, to let Winthrop see better. Tiger's reason, because Frank told him to slouch low. Winthrop knew he could have let Frank handle this one but he had a personal stake in what happened. No one hung up in his ear. He didn't enjoy it and wanted to discuss it, at some painful length, with the punk who'd done it.

Inside the open doors of the pier shed, ten of Winthrop's soldiers waited. Parked on Delaware Avenue were six more, two in each of a pair of wheelless hulks abandoned there and another two in the door wells of a Trailways bus with a broken rear axle. A total of sixteen shivering men waited for Mike Bradley. The night threatened snow and delivered a chilling mist, unpleasant enough to make passersby want to keep passing by yet not thick enough to conceal the scene from Winthrop's observation post. In spite of his irritation he was almost pleased by the weather. He couldn't have arranged it better himself. Nor could he have chosen a better meeting site. The smart-mouth on the phone had talked himself into a real bind, picking this spot. Small ironies like that pleased Theodore Winthrop, who ticked off items ranked on his mental list of preparations. Foolproof. He would have the thief in minutes, and then most of the night to persuade this moron of the error of his ways. He tugged at his pigskin gloves and waited.

At 10:00 PM a man on a Piaggio scooter rode past the entrance to Pier 30, slowing as he passed. Winthrop leaned forward, anticipating, but slumped back again when the scooter continued north. Then it stopped, swung in a circle, and returned. The man stopped outside the open pier shed and parked his scooter. He looked around for a moment, stepped into a pool of light under the street lamp, and seemed to be reading something. He might not be the one. Then he walked into the darkness inside the shed.

The trap sprung.

Six men jumped from their hiding places on the street and dashed into the darkened shed after the man. The doors slid shut behind them, and the shed remained dark. It was a dead end. With only that single door for an exit and sixteen men surrounding him, the smart-mouth was finished. Winthrop knew his trap might seem extreme to some, like hunting mice with a rocket launcher. But he had got where he was by being thorough, not by worrying about what people thought of his methods.

He leaned forward to tap Frank Guappo on the shoulder. "That's it. Let's go talk to him."

Frank straightened up in the seat and had time to say "Tiger . . . " before both back doors of the limousine flew open and two men lunged into the car, one from each side.

"Hold it!" one of them shouted. "One move and Aiello bleeds all over this pretty car!" He held a long, glittering knife, the cold metal blade denting the flesh of Winthrop's neck short of breaking the skin. (A butter knife should stop short of breaking the skin, but only Mike Bradley knew that . . . Mike hoped.) "Nobody move even a little bit! Tell them!" The cold blade Aiello could feel but couldn't see pushed a touch harder.

"Sit still," Winthrop whispered. "Don't do anything, Frank." He glanced to both sides without turning his head. The knife blade flickered in the light of the streetlamp outside. The hand holding it against the left side of his neck wore a rubber glove. While Winthrop tried not to move, the man on his right reached over to release two buttons of Winthrop's topcoat, then tugged and slid the half-buttoned coat down over his arms to trap him. Winthrop turned to steal a look at the face on his left . . . and knew instantly how little good that would do him.

His attacker wore a muffler and hat to conceal his features. What wasn't concealed was distorted, like a character from one of those alien movies—misshapen and otherworldly, in his appearance more unnerving than the knife he wielded. Knives, Winthrop understood, and nothing he understood frightened him very much. Uncertainty was another matter. In appearance the knife-wielder was so far outside Winthrop's experience that he represented uncertainty.

"You two in front, look straight ahead and don't make a sound." The man holding the knife did the talking. He twisted around on the seat till his face was inches from Aiello's. "That was a mistake, wasn't it? An innocent messenger boy came to deliver a note to you, and what thanks did he get? I counted six of your goons going in after him. Were there many inside waiting?"

Winthrop stared at the face without answering. The longer they sat here, the better he liked it. Three pros against two amateurs. That difference, and time to let these strangers make a slip, were in his favor.

"You'll be lucky if the boy doesn't die of fright. But I'm depending on your careful instructions. You did tell your men not to hurt him till you got there, didn't you?"

Again, Winthrop waited. When neither of the eerie figures spoke further, he said, "You're the one making the mistake. And it's a big one."

Mike Bradley twitched the knife and watched Aiello's eyes close. Aiello might be tough, but he was scared, too. "Let me guess. You didn't bring the money, did you?"

"Not a cent."

"Twice you've tried cheating. You're a hard man to trust."

"Keep talking, punk."

"We'll go get it then. You two in front, let me have your names."

"Tiger Guappo."

Frank said, "Stuff it."

"It doesn't matter, Frank." Winthrop spoke with his eyes closed. "Tell him."

Sullen, Frank said, "You heard him. It's Frank. I'm Frank Guappo."

"Never heard of you," Mike said. "So you'll get out here, Frank. I need an errand boy. First, you walk down to the pier and tell your friends there—"

"In a pig's ass."

"Uhhh!" Aiello flinched as the dull knife point twitched and he imagined a bead of blood. "Frank! Do what he says!"

"That's right, Frank. You do what I say. You walk down to the pier and tell your friends they're through for the night. I want them to leave and head straight for the parking lot at Penn's Landing. We've got two men watching that lot. They want to see it filling up before I turn your boss loose. Got that?"

"Uh-huh."

"Speak up, Frank. Have you got that?"

"I heard you!" Frank turned in the seat to say something else but snapped his head front when he saw the knife.

"That's better. Now, after those people leave, you get in touch with your watchdogs. I want them off the bridge approaches. All three bridges."

"I don't know what—"

"Aiello?" Mike tapped him with the knife.

"For Christ's sake, Frank! Don't argue!"

Mike switched hands on the knife handle. Inside the rubber glove his right hand was sweating and his arm trembled with tension. His tough-guy act sounded absurd even to him, but he couldn't drop it. "That's it. You call off the men at the bridges, and they go out to the parking lot, too. We've got the cars counted, including the two at the Franklin Bridge. My men will signal me when your guys are all at the stadium."

It was silent in the car, except for a muted sneeze from the silent one beside Aiello. He sneezed, twitched, but didn't loosen his grip on Aiello's bunched topcoat.

"What are you waiting for, Frank?" Mike asked. "See you at Penn's Landing. We'll deliver your boss there in an hour, if he doesn't try anything stupid in the meantime."

"I'll be waiting," Frank said. "Frank Guappo. Remember the name."

"Uh-huh. Nice gesture, you got me scared. Now move it."

Frank got out of the car and started down the sloping street at a trot, turning up his collar and running with hunched shoulders like a man wearing a bullseye on his back.

"Now," Mike said. "Let's get to the money. No, don't argue. To you, thirty thousand is nothing, fifteen hundred a car. It's not worth bleeding over, is it?"

Winthrop said, "Drive where he tells you, Tiger." He twisted his head to watch Mike's face as he spoke. "There's about ten thousand in the glove compartment. Take that and get out."

"Take it!" Harry hissed. "Let's do what he—"

"Shut up, Howard!" Mike snapped.

"Howard?" Harry glanced over his shoulder in bewilderment.

Winthrop smiled. "Howard's right," he said easily. "Ten thousand, and I let you walk away free. That's more money than you ever held in your life, punk."

"I think I'd rather have the ten plus thirty, without your permission to walk away. You're lucky I don't raise the ante after that cute play down there at the pier." Mike's voice took on a note of mock sorrow. "I don't think I can trust a man who doesn't keep appointments."

"I notice you weren't down there, either."

"Yours was dishonesty, mine was caution. . . . Tiger, are you driving this hearse or not?"

Tiger started the engine and guided the limousine slowly down the street. As they passed Frank at the foot of the slope Tiger tooted the horn and waved at his brother. "Hey, Frank!"

"Shut up, Tiger." Winthrop closed his eyes again. After a moment's thought he said, "Take us to Barney's. He'll give you the money."

"Yes sir."

"Shut up, Tiger."

The limousine moved through the damp streets toward South Philadelphia.

Harry leaned forward to look at Mike past Aiello's paralysis. "Radio?"

"That's right," Mike said. "We don't want to forget that little detail, do we." He knew he shouldn't be talking so much but something in the air, the tension or fear that he kept suppressed, had him feeling garrulous. "Tiger, turn on that talk show. What's the station, Howard?"

"You mean WCAU?" Tiger said to help.

Harry hunched over the front seat to watch Tiger fumble for the radio switch. "Hey look! There's a phone up there. A teeny little phone, right in the car."

Mike smiled. "A bonus." He nudged Aiello's arm. "You don't mind if we use it, do you?"

Winthrop said nothing. In the faint flow of streetlights flitting past he studied his captor's face. It was no longer ominous. A simple disguise, randomly drawn black lines cross-hatching the nose and cheeks, some kind of makeup it looked like, and over it all a nylon stocking pulled taut. The man's nose was flattened and spread, lips pulled back in a permanent grimace, eyes widened till they seemed oriental. He looked like a death's head.

So did the man on his right. Winthrop couldn't account for the judgment he made but he knew that the one with the knife was the younger, probably no more than thirty; the other one, now, he was older. Say, in his fifties. Winthrop had that much to go on, and he could listen to their voices. If he walked away from this car, he would have something about them to remember, no matter how long it took to find them.

"Close your eyes," Mike said. "Not that staring will do you much good. I don't get to Philly that often, and after tonight you'll never see me again."

"After tonight, nobody'll see you again," Winthrop said. But he closed his eyes. The voices would be enough, now. Whoever these two were—"Howard" and the nameless one—they weren't local. Several clues suggested that. He knew all the local pros, and these two looked less and less like amateurs as time passed: their disguises were simple but effective, they'd ambushed him, and they weren't fooling with small fry, as amateurs might. Beyond that, nobody local said "Philly," any more than a native San Franciscan could say "Frisco" without choking.

In a few minutes the limousine swung south off Snyder and stopped in front of a small bar. "We're here," Tiger said.

"Tell Barney I want thirty thousand out of his safe, and if he argues or asks any questions, you tell him Frank will come and persuade him, you understand that?"

"I understand that."

"And hurry," Harry said, wheezing.

"I understand that," Tiger said.

Mike said. "My arm's getting tired. I don't want to slip, or be so surprised that I make any sudden moves."

"I understand that."

The street was dark, the inside of the parked limousine darker yet. Still, Mike pushed Aiello back against the seat. Switching the knife to his right hand again, he reached past Aiello's still form and clasped Harry's left hand with his own. They pressed Aiello back into the comfortable cushions and sat waiting. Only the car radio broke the silence. A long argument about the Phillies' winter trades was underway, and Harry had no interest in baseball, so only three-fourths of his attention focused on the radio frequency numbers glowing LED-orange in the dashboard. Part of him stayed on the job in the backseat, keeping Aiello quiet.

"Your goon better hurry," Mike said.

"Getting edgy?" Aiello smiled, his eyes still closed. "You took on too big a job this time, and you can't stand the heat."

Mike craned his neck to check Aiello's wristwatch. Three minutes since Tiger had entered the bar but it seemed much longer. He knew Aiello was right and didn't like to admit it, even to himself. Inside the stocking mask he could feel sweat trickling into his eyes. He blinked to clear them. The nylon pantyhose leg pulled at him and made him itch, no matter how he made faces and twisted his mouth to shift the binding cloth and seek relief. He fought off the urge to switch hands with the knife again. It seemed another ten minutes had passed, and still no Tiger.

"You hear that?" Harry said. "Bring back Robin Roberts, for God's sake! The man must be eighty by now. If they—"

"Howard! Knock it off! Just listen." Mike heard the edge in his own voice and hoped Aiello couldn't know how close he was to cracking.

The bar door swung open and Tiger appeared in the light carrying a canvas bag big enough for a pair of bowling shoes. He slid in behind the wheel and turned around to look back at them. "Barney don't like it. He said it's not safe to carry so much—"

"Go!" Mike said. "Get moving!"

Tiger dropped the bag to the seat beside him and pulled away from the curb.

"Now where?" Winthrop asked. His confidence was returning. Nothing had happened to him yet, and he could feel the tension building on both sides of him. His captors were more nervous than he was. They had a problem he didn't share, if they were as smart as they seemed: they wanted to end the night without anyone getting hurt. He wanted to hurt someone.

"Straight ahead," Mike said. "I'll tell you where."

They rode in silence for several blocks, till Mike said, "There! Stop the car." He let go of Harry's hand and switched the knife, with his free hand pointing ahead of them at a phone booth on the street corner. "Stop here, Tiger. And Howard, you make that call we talked about. The first one. Our friends are waiting."

"It's raining out there!" Harry protested. "Why don't I use the car phone?"

"Because mobile calls are easy to trace. Isn't that right?" Mike nudged Aiello with his elbow.

"Do your own thinking. I'll do mine."

The car stopped, and still Harry grumbled. He was feeling a chill, he said, the stocking itched; but Mike cut him off, and Harry climbed from the car in patient martyrdom.

Lee sat shivering in the dark truck cab. She had shifted through the gears several times, matching her actions to the diagram above her head. "Spicer-seven," she read. It meant nothing. She thought she could handle the truck, but thinking it and doing it weren't the same thing. She was amazed to find herself sitting here, waiting. Paulie had paid their motel bill for another night in case the call from Harry didn't come through and they were forced to hunker down right here. Now he crouched in the phone booth beside the manager's cabin at the Hi-Way House Rest Stop with the door open to prevent the overhead light from giving him away. Lee knew he was there but she couldn't see him. It had started to rain. She wasn't sure whether the windshield wipers would work without the engine running and didn't want to chance trying them. She sat slumped and waited.

The phone booth blazed light as Paulie pulled the door shut behind him. Lee could see him holding the receiver and nodding. The light went out and Paulie ran past her truck to his, pounding on the door as he went by.

"We go!" he shouted.

Lee twisted together the wires as Paulie had shown her and the engine caught with a deep roar. She led the way past the neon lights of the motel out onto the highway.

Harry tried entering Mike's side of the car, but Tiger said, "Sheeesh!" and waved him away. "You're sitting on the other side, Howard. Remember?"

"They're coming," Harry said, as he got back into Aiello's Cadillac.

Mike felt himself relax. "There you are. Your cars are on the way back."

"From Jersey?" Winthrop asked. The question was too casual.

"You knew that."

"How did you know I knew that?"

Mike shook his head. "Okay, Tiger. One more little trip, and you can have the rest of the day off. Start for Center City, but take Delaware Avenue in. We're going to the bridge to wait for some friends." Mike reached over with his free hand to slide Aiello's sleeve back and check the time. 10:35. Lee and Paulie would be crossing the bridge by 11:00. "Time for your next call," he said, and grinned as Harry jumped.

"Now? You sure?"

"You've been waiting. Use that one."

Nodding, Harry reached into the front seat to snatch the folded phone from its cradle. "How do I . . . ?" He looked at the empty cradle, the phone in his hand, then located the pad of numbered buttons. He punched in a number he'd memorized years ago but had never called. He leaned back. "We might have to wait. Some of them complain like hell how long they wait."

"Howard? Don't talk so much. Just remember your lines." Mike glanced at Aiello, who sat with his eyes closed and registered no emotion.

The car crept back toward the center of Philadelphia, with only the noise of the radio to cover the heavy rasp of their breathing in the quiet car. Tiger drove with his head locked straight ahead, signaling at each turn, and pushing the quiet limousine through the wet streets with surprising grace and care. No one spoke. They watched the receiver in Harry's hand, and waited.

Winthrop said, "I don't know who you're phoning, but it won't help. Why not call this off before—"

"Never give up, do you?" Mike said with a chuckle in his voice.

"Don't patronize me, you punk!" Winthrop let his anger flare for an instant, then regained control. "Never mind. I've said all I'm going to say. Until the next time we meet."

"Sure. Hold that thought."

"Hello? Is this . . . Hello?" Harry held the phone in front of him and started at it as if it were alive. His own voice sounded over the car radio, delayed as the station's loop-tape recorded and played him back. Another voice—the announcer's—said, "If you've got your radio on, will you turn it down, please? You're on the air."

Tiger glanced back to say, "They always tell you that, Howard. Turn down your radio, they tell you. You should know that." He turned the volume down and said, "Tsk, tsk, tsk."

"Hello? . . . Am I on yet? . . . Yes, well about what you were saying before. . . . " Harry panicked and turned to Mike for help.

"Tell him!" Mike whispered. "And Tiger, turn that radio back up."

"You shouldn't have the sound on when you're—"

"Turn it up!"

"No," Harry said into the telephone. "Nothing's wrong. I just wanted to say, all your listeners are going to be surprised. There's a bomb in City Hall set to go off in twenty-five minutes. Got it? Twenty-five minutes... Hello?"

Tiger spun the volume control in time for them to hear: "...bomb in City Hall set to go—Sorry, folks, another practical joker. I don't know why I get them all. Now, if anyone has a question for Phillies' manager—"

"Turn it off," Mike said. "And stop the car."

Winthrop's eyes were open, squinting, focused on Mike. This new ploy puzzled him, but he would wait and understand it. Pros, not amateurs, he decided, and imaginative as well. As much as he hated to give them credit, he had to admit that. He sat glancing from Mike to Harry while Mike rolled down the window. Then an idea struck. "Remember what you said about mobile calls? They'll trace that to my car!"

"You'll think of something to tell them," Mike said.

"But if the cops—"

"Quiet!"

Harry had forgotten about Aiello beside him. He scratched at his face with both gloved hands, twisting the pantyhose mask and smearing the eyebrow pencil under it, all the while smiling and muttering, "They heard me. I guess I told them that time. Idiots! Nothing to talk about but baseball. They all heard me."

The temperature stood at eighty-four humid degrees, the last gasp of a dying air conditioning system inside Police Headquarters, in Center City Philadelphia, in the distinctive building that Philadelphians call The Roundhouse.

The air was warmer than the night air on the streets outside and at least as humid. Patrolman Warren Cappel had indigestion, three hours to go on a five-hour shift as temporary desk sergeant, transferred in off the street by a merciful watch commander because of a rash that made him lean back in his swivel chair every few minutes to scratch his crotch like a major league batter unaware of the TV camera.

He didn't enjoy desk duty. His rash hadn't healed and in fact was tougher to scratch when he sat on it. On the street he ticketed some law-breakers, ignored others, and was lord of his own destiny. Or at least lord of his summons pad. He could walk away from issues he didn't like or understand. But here, fifteen feet inside The Roundhouse main doorway, he had no choices at all. Every drunk, every hooker, every villain, miscreant, offender, suspect, and lost citizen looking for help, protection, or redress, walked up to his desk.

And between their irritating and confusing demands, the phone rang. Somewhere in the bowels of The Roundhouse was a switchboard whose two operators routed calls to the duty emergency catcher, the 911 action squad, any department personnel asked for by name, or—when the issue wasn't clear—to Patrolman Warren Cappel. Himself.

So, when the phone rang at 10:42 PM, he reached for the receiver in dread, scratched with the other hand, and said, "What's it about?"

"What?"

"Police Duty Desk, what's the problem?"

The man on the line claimed to be the night producer at some radio station. Warren Cappel didn't get the call letters, but they would be on the tape that recorded every message. "We got a call," he said, "and it sounds like the real thing. A bomb in City Hall, set to blow in twenty minutes."

"Oh shit!" Officer Cappel hit the panic button and set in motion the bomb squad emergency sequence. Then, while he returned to the phone to copy details, The Roundhouse danced with activity unsuspected only moments before: officers donned protective gear, ran to their cars, the street outside chaotic as vehicles boiled up out of the basement garage onto Locust in a siren-screaming stream of flashing lights and squealing tires headed for City Hall twelve blocks away.

At least Warren Cappel didn't have to go with them. He could stay in comparative peace, pencil in his right hand, scratching with his left. Routine resumed for Officer Warren Cappel. The city was safe in his capable hands. Capable hand.

"Shhh!" Mike sat with his neck craned and listened. His posture made the others imitate him. The limo had stopped at the foot of Main, and off to their left sirens built volume. First one, then a second, soon a whole chorus of sirens sounded through the city. A squad car coming hard behind them careened left onto Main with lights flashing and screamed toward City Hall.

"Get to the bridge!" Mike said, and thumped Tiger on the back of the head, in his excitement leaning forward and letting the knife drift clear of Aiello's neck.

Winthrop lunged past Harry and threw the door open before Mike and Harry could react. Harry seized him and wrestled with him hanging half out the open door, as Tiger floored the accelerator and the limousine careened up Delaware Avenue and slammed into a wrenching left turn that kept the open door swinging, Harry and Aiello swaying out over the cobblestoned street. Mike lunged for the pair and felt cold mist spray his face; he tangled his fingers in Aiello's hair and got a grip with the other hand on the man's topcoat to keep him from spilling out onto the street. Harry yelled something unintelligible and waved one hand in the air, groping for safety as the cobblestones flashed past beneath him, till the car completed the turn and righted itself.

"Get him back in here!" Mike shouted, and helped Harry prop Aiello erect. Out of breath and shaking, he jabbed his prisoner with the dull knife again, wondering as he did how long he could get away with the bluff. "Don't make me do it," he said. "I'm a little shaky right now. Don't you move even a finger."

Winthrop froze against the seat cushions with his eyes closed and sat stone-still, as if he hadn't moved at all. He was panting but regained his composure.

Harry tugged the heavy door shut and scratched at his nylon stocking mask. Tiger swung right onto Locust headed toward the bridge.

After the blast of cool air from the open door the car felt stifling and smelled like a locker room. Mike worked the fingers on his free hand and wrung out his tension, saying nothing, letting Tiger go, waiting till they were on the bridge itself and halfway up the sloping western side. "Stop!" he shouted.

Tiger said, "You can't stop on the bridge."

"Stop the car!"

"I'll get a ticket."

"Stop the car, or I throw your boss out. I mean it!"

Tiger slammed on the brakes, hurling Harry to the floor and forcing Mike to grab Aiello in a bear hug to steady them both. He clawed blindly along the floor and retrieved the fallen knife, but Aiello ignored the moment. He'd made his bid to escape and now sat quiet. Cars following them swerved past with horns fading dopplers into the distance. Behind them sirens still sounded. Through the back window Mike could see the flashing lights of fire engines and rescue squad trucks crossing the bridge approach as they headed south from Police Headquarters toward City Hall.

"Right here. We wait right here."

Tiger tried to be reasonable. "You know you can't stop in traffic like this, and you can't stop on a bridge. I already told you that before. You'll get a ticket." It was his longest speech in months and gave him a headache.

Mike laughed. "A ticket? From who? Every cop within ten miles is headed for City Hall by now. Don't worry about tickets. We'll sit here, and wait."

Winthrop opened his eyes to stare at Mike. He seemed on the verge of a question but then shrugged. Answers would come later. He could wait.

In spite of the work it took to maneuver the truck and turn the stiff steering wheel, Lee found the drive through Camden to the Ben Franklin Bridge anticlimactic. She got the hang of shifting through the gears and discovered that she could manipulate the clutch well enough by sitting forward on the seat. She didn't know what a

"Spicerthisorthat" was but could work the damn thing, and her weight leaning against the steering wheel helped dampen out some of its shimmying.

She led Paulie into the right lane at the bridge and the bored attendant didn't bother to look at her. She might just as well have come without the mustache that tickled her nose into a constant rabbit twitch.

Paulie followed her without incident, and they drove over the bridge in a gentle rain that gave a misted halo to each of the overhead lights sliding past like amber streaks smeared on the night sky.

For more than six minutes, Aiello's limousine sat parked upslope on the Pennsylvania side of the bridge, the object of shouted anger from motorists forced to swerve around it on their way by. To Mike Bradley the six minutes seemed more like an hour. Harry had become useless and might have been alone in the car, for all the attention he paid to the others. He sneezed more often now, and muttered about pneumonia, all the while scratching his face. Mike's patience was pushing its limit when he spotted Lee's car carrier headed toward them.

"There they are!" Harry shouted.

Winthrop flinched and said, "Shut him up!"

Crossing the crest of the bridge, headed their way, were Paulie and Lee with their dancing, swaying loads. Mike reached forward to honk the horn and earned waves of recognition from the mustached figures hauling the Cadillacs back into Philadelphia.

"Climb in front," Mike ordered Harry. "And Tiger, you move this mother! NOW!"

Harry clambered up beside Tiger and clasped the canvas bag of money to his chest as the limousine lurched squealing into the flow of traffic.

"Faster," Mike shouted. "All she's got!"

They hit 50 MPH at the crest of the bridge, with a widening gap of a hundred yards between them and the nearest set of headlights trailing them.

"STOP!" Mike yelled. "STOP IT!" and in the same breath reached past Aiello to hurl open the curbside door. The car skewed to a shuddering stop canted across two lanes and Mike pushed Aiello from the car, leaned over Tiger to open the driver's door, and shoved Tiger sprawling to the pavement. He scrambled over the seat back, clouting Harry in the head with his foot on the way, and slipped under the wheel, dropped the gearshift lever into low and stood on the accelerator, cramping the wheel left. They made a shimmying, squealing turn on the bridge mere feet ahead of following traffic and cut between two white-eyed drivers headed upslope from the Jersey side. Mike passed one on the outside, cut inside the other, topped the crest of the bridge and pushed the car to 70 MPH heading down the closed center lanes back toward Philadelphia.

The Christmas Tree of lights on the second car carrier showed the truck reaching the corner of Locust and turning left on its way to The Roundhouse and Police Headquarters.

Nearing the foot of the bridge Mike slammed the brake pedal down and heard Harry thump against the dashboard to his right. "Money, Harry!" he shouted. "In the glove compartment. Get that other money!"

They rolled off the bridge onto Vine Street at a sedate 30 MPH. Across the park to his left Mike could see the tail end of the first car carrier drop over a dip and duck into the police garage under The Roundhouse. The second truck was right behind it.

Lee felt the lip of the garage threshold throw her off the seat for an instant but she held the wheel and braced for a jolt at the bottom. It came, and she bounced level again in the glare of white lights. Hulking concrete pillars on both sides marked a long lane to the end of the garage where two empty squad cars sat parked. She never got that far. No idea what lay ahead of her, she stomped on the emergency brake as the truck leveled out in the police garage and felt it stagger to a bucking stop, cramped in an L. The engine shuddered and died at the sudden stop in gear. She used her baseball cap to scrub prints off the steering wheel and smear the door handle as she jumped down from the cab.

Paulie's truck slid in behind hers and Paulie was out and running. She stripped off her mustache, shook free her tangled hair, and reached out to grab Paulie's hand. He pulled her up the garage ramp as fast as they could run.

Mike made two left turns, Vine onto 7th and 7th onto Locust, glancing at Harry to make certain the ten thousand dollars from the glove compartment got stuffed into the bowling shoe bag. He stopped Aiello's limousine in a No Parking Zone in front of the police Roundhouse.

He and Harry jumped from the car just as Paulie and Lee sprinted into sight from the underground police garage. Together, the four of them dashed through traffic across Locust and into the park, where Harry stopped to stand splayfooted, stripping off his mask and gloves.

"Not now, not yet!" Mike said, and grabbed Harry's arm to pull him through the park. They ran to the Vine Street side where the beige Honda sat under a street lamp. Breathless and gasping they clambered into the car and pulled away. Their wheezing turned to broken laughter. Mike stripped loose his gloves and tugged the nylon stockings off over this head, then both he and Harry set to work scrubbing at the smeared streaks of eyebrow pencil with cold cream and tissues Lee pushed into their reaching hands.

"God! You should have seen it!" Paulie leaned forward from the backseat and pounded Mike's shoulders. "That whole garage, empty! Not a cop in sight. It was beautiful! Wait'll they find those carriers in there."

Lee joined him in hanging over the back of the front seats and kissed her father on the neck. "What do you think now, Daddy?"

Harry hoisted the canvas bag and grinned. His first relaxed smile in weeks. "I'm using my money and going to Hawaii." Then he sneezed. Twice. "I think I caught a cold," he complained. "And Mike kicked me in the ear."

The other three hooted him down, till Lee said, "Wait!" She peered at her father. "What happened to you, Daddy? You're all broken out."

In the dim overhead light the others looked at a red rash that covered Harry from the top of his cinched muffler to his receding hairline. He squirmed to the side and examined himself in the rearview mirror. When he spoke, his voice was filled with wonder. "Nylons. I'm allergict to nylons! I mean, really allergict!"

Most of the night they spent celebrating. By 4:00 AM a fifty-five-gallon drum placed in the middle of Paulie's empty warehouse floor held the ashes of their shredded clothes, melted gloves, crisp fragments of burned stockings, anything that might link them to the twenty Cadillacs ranked on the carriers and parked in The Roundhouse underground garage. Mike persuaded Paulie to stick with the job at Heritage, at least till they could arrange the showing of Paulie's designs. They vowed to let life go on as usual, no changes, nothing to indicate the comparative wealth they shared. And with all those vows, they burst into laughter whenever Lee winked at one of them. Lee and Mike took Harry home to a hot bath and some Dristan. Each carried a small paper sack of ashes. They drove with the car windows open, scattering ashes on the breeze of their passage through the dark Philadelphia streets.

MONDAY

On the conference table at Heritage Old-Line Fidelity Insurance Monday morning lay fifteen calf-bound notebooks. Inside each were an estate-planning kit and a gold-filled ballpoint pen; on the cover of each notebook, embossed in gold, was the name of a proud graduate. One difference in the room: at the far end were three rows of folding chairs filled with family. Mothers in dresses and fathers in suits. Here and there was a son or daughter, restless and bored with the pre-ceremony wait, as they would be by the ceremony to come. Lee was there, and Harry, wearing an aloha shirt under his raccoon coat and planning his trip on a yellow legal pad.

Mike Bradley sat at the table and scanned the other trainees' faces with bleary eyes. Paulie Klein and Robert Boyle were late or missing, though only one notebook remained to be claimed. It was labeled "Paul Joseph Klein" and lay to Mike's right. Boyle hadn't made it through the training program, a fact that brightened the day for Mike, as if the day needed brightening. He was smiling, pleased with himself, with Weiss' good judgment in failing Boyle, with the world in general, with the fact that Lee had come along today of her own choice. And she hadn't said no when his most recent proposal followed their lovemaking this morning. She'd only hummed and kissed his cheek. Humming was halfway to yes.

Paulie came bounding in with a folded newspaper in his hand. "Have you seen it?" he whispered as he flopped into his chair. "All over the front page." He spread the paper on the table and leaned back to watch Mike read. He caught Lee's eye and waved a greeting.

Headlines announced the bomb scare, and beneath them parallel columns—two stories—recounted the massive search of City Hall the night before and the mystery of $750,000 worth of Detroit tin abandoned in the police garage. Theories abounded in reports untainted by facts. One columnist explained, without suggesting a source for his certainty, that the unknown thieves had suffered a sudden twinge of conscience and decided to return their loot before anyone knew in fact that he'd been robbed. King Kolchak was quoted; what he said was unclear and therefore perfectly in character. Near the bottom of the page, two of the Cadillac owners were pictured standing beside the loaded car carriers pointing at their own cars. The entire front page of the *Inquirer*'s early edition was entertaining without being informative. Quite a spread.

Mike skimmed through it smiling, at the same time restraining Paulie who bounced with delight in the chair next to his.

"Aiello's got pull all right," Mike said. "His name's left out of it."

Paulie said, "I didn't think of that," and leaned close to glance through the stories again.

Mike flipped to page eight as the leather-padded doors at the front of the room opened and Carleton Weiss entered. Mike folded his newspaper into a small square and slipped it beneath the tabletop onto his lap where he could read it unnoticed. Almost like being back in college: a prof droning at the front of the room, the sports page at hand.

"It's been a good week," Weiss began.

Paulie Klein choked back a laugh and punched Mike's arm.

"You all came through with your colors flying, so to speak. I'm not one to give speeches"—Weiss looked over his shoulder, cocked an ear toward the door, checked his watch, cleared his throat—"but I see we have a few minutes and I want to talk serious-wise about something. Now, we've had a lot of fun together these past few days, but I don't want you to get the idea that the insurance game is nothing but fun. There'll be hard work ahead of you, and disappointments. I think you've all got the stuff to take it. It won't be as bad as it was in the old days, when I got my start. I can remember . . ."

Mike focused on the folded newspaper in his lap. A pair of sidebars on page eight added little to the front-page stories. The first contained a brief interview with one Leslie Harp, a woman in Upper Darby who had a week earlier dreamt about stolen cars being abandoned in the police garage. Her dream matched the actual event in elaborate detail, including the precise colors of all twenty cars (Desert Wind, Northern Frost, Cinnabar, and so on). To authenticate the woman's story, the reporter conducting the interview included several confirming comments from the woman's nine-year-old daughter, who vouched for her mother's honesty. There were also references to Nostradamus and Jeanne Dixon.

The second sidebar was more cryptic. To Mike it seemed unrelated to the main story of the day. The limousine of financier Theodore Winthrop was found parked in a No Parking Zone outside The Roundhouse, and Winthrop had no explanation for its presence there, except to assume that some joyriding kids had stolen and then abandoned it. "What's this about Winthrop's car? Why would Aiello come to the meet last night in a stolen limo?" he whispered to Paulie.

"What?"

The padded double doors swung open with a thud and silenced Weiss. A murmur of conversation marked the moment but ceased as soon as everyone categorized the man who came through the doorway. He was uninteresting. Only a photographer, covered with strap-hung cameras, a light meter, and other arcane paraphernalia.

Weiss cleared his throat and launched into another actuarial history, and his audience sagged in their chairs to resume glazed boredom. All except Mike Bradley.

Because hard on the photographer's heels came Frank and Tiger Guappo in their wide floral ties. They slipped into the room and very visibly feigned invisibility. They stood motionless. Tiger sported a pair of Band-Aid strips across his forehead, evidence of his collision with the pavement the night before. Frank looked drained. Details of a sleepless night weren't specified on his face but obviously something had kept him from his bed. He showed slits for eyes in a pneumatic gray face. The two brothers bracketed the doorway like sentinels, and Mike fought the urge to bolt from the room.

Paulie Klein sensed his tension. "What's the matter, man?"

"We may have a problem. Watch me."

Seated among the spectators at the end of the room, Harry Schaeffer glanced up from his legal pad, recognized the Guappos, and blanched. He ducked into his collar and spoke to Lee beside him. Both of them looked to Mike for a clue but he shook his head in warning. Lee pulled Harry close and they conferred in anxious whispers.

"What is it?" Paulie was insistent. "You okay?"

Mike felt his calves tense as he came a preparatory inch off his chair and held his unnoticed crouch like a sprinter in the starting blocks. He didn't know which way to run but something was wrong.

"It's coming apart!" he said to Paulie.

"And now the moment you've all been waiting for," Weiss said, recapturing their attention. "It is my honor and privilege to introduce this year's graduates of the Heritage Old-Line Fidelity training and development program.... You may applaud."

Most did. Mike didn't. Mind racing, he sought to understand their dilemma at the same time he debated escape routes. There weren't any that didn't pass between the Guappo brothers guarding the exit—a short, deadly gantlet to run. Sweat trickled down the small of his back and both palms itched.

"Richard Abbott," Weiss intoned, reading from a list. "Please present yourself for your well-deserved recognition."

A smattering of uncertain applause greeted "Ohio State," who walked forward wearing a mantle of sheepish pride to accept his engraved certificate of completion and Carleton Weiss' meaty handshake.

The photographer took a picture, muttered "One more," and his flash flared again.

"Stewart F. Barnes," Weiss said, beckoning the next graduate. Another presentation, another pair of photos.

Paulie said, "Abbott, Barnes . . . sounds alphabetical. The dork from Williams, that Boyle guy, is next. Then you."

But Weiss called out, "Esther Flett, with a near-perfect score on her final exam! My personal congratulations, Mizz Flett."

Esther stood to accept her certificate and winked at Mike and Paulie, bending slightly to whisper as she walked past, "Fooled his honky ass, didn't I?"

Paulie shook her hand and turned to Mike, "He skipped over you. What's going on?"

"What?"

"Get with the program, man! You're daydreaming while your lady there wants to cheer for you." He nodded toward Lee, who was smiling in anticipation.

"Robert Inkster," Weiss read.

Paulie was offended. "Isn't he going to call you?"

"Wait and see." He kept close watch on Frank Guappo.

"Something's screwed up."

"Paul Joseph Klein." Weiss motioned for Paulie to approach.

Lee whistled a shrill two-finger blast of celebration that drew all eyes her way. She blushed in the empathetic laughter and nudged Harry, who only pushed his earplug tighter and hid from the Guappo brothers within the comforting circle of his unseen friends on talk radio.

Paulie waved thanks to Lee and ambled to the front of the room with a broad smile in place.

Tiger Guappo joined in the general applause for each graduate. Easy to get started, he was less easy to stop. Each time applause faded away and Tiger was the only one whose solitary handclaps punctuated the silence, Frank seized Tiger's wrists to stop him.

Weiss read through thirteen names, omitting Boyle, who had failed the program, and Mike Bradley. When Weiss was clearly finished but somehow wasn't yet done, a murmur rose from the spectators.

And that's when the pieces came together. Tiger Guappo sucked in his stomach; Frank straightened his shoulders; Carleton Weiss peered out the open doors into the hallway; and Mike Bradley sank back onto his chair at seeing Pete Aiello stride impressively into the room.

"That's torn it," Mike whispered.

"Who's the guy?"

Weiss beamed and held out a hand, palm-up, to introduce, "Our President, Mr. Theodore Winthrop."

"Winthrop?" Mike said aloud.

"Are you Michael Bradley? I heard about you." Winthrop beckoned. "Up here."

In the rank of folding chairs, Lee tugged at Harry's coat sleeve and drew him slowly to his feet. Something was wrong, she didn't know what, and she waited for Mike's cue.

"That's you!" Paulie said, urging Mike to his feet.

"First in his class," Weiss intoned. "Michael Alan Bradley."

Praying silently that his stocking mask had been effective, Mike brazened it out and walked up to take Winthrop's outstretched hand. He didn't mind the grip he met, so long as it was Winthrop and not Pietro Aiello who seized his hand.

Flashbulbs flared. Lee sidled toward the exit door towing Harry, who tucked his face even deeper into his fur collar. There was grudging applause for Mike from the other trainees, a more generous response from family members in the audience, and true enthusiasm from Tiger Guappo.

"Knock it off, Tiger," Frank said.

"'Scuse us," Harry muttered, pushing between the Guappos, who had closed ranks at the doorway and were watching their boss for instructions.

"That's okay, Howard," Tiger said, stepping aside and nodding to Harry in recognition.

Frank said, "Shut up, Tiger."

Winthrop congratulated Mike, who mumbled something and tried to walk away. Winthrop clung to his hand. "Have we met somewhere?" he asked. His question was light and curious, not a threat. "Recently?"

"Doubt it," Mike said, in the hoarsest voice he could contrive. "I spent the whole weekend in bed. Flu." He pulled his hand away and coughed into it. But as he did, he felt a wave of comfort wash over him. In a burst of elation he understood Aiello's persona and alias and almost laughed aloud as he said, "No problem."

"What's that?" Winthrop asked.

"How about another?" Mike pulled Winthrop to his left side, Weiss to his right, and hugged them with camaraderie. "Want to get this?" he asked the photographer.

Paulie Klein clapped louder than anyone as the flash flared again and recorded on film a three-person photo....

One that Carleton Weiss these days always points out to new recruits in the Heritage Old-Line Fidelity Insurance Company underwriter trainee classes. "That's me with our founder, Theodore Winthrop. The young guy there in the middle is Mike Bradley. First in his class, runs the Wilmington office now, partner in a trucking agency over in Jersey somewhere, doing great. A real pro."